Death of a
Thin-skinned Animal

Death of a Thin-skinned Animal

Patrick Alexander

E. P. DUTTON

NEW YORK

First American edition published 1977 by E.P. Dutton,
a Division of Sequoia-Elsevier Publishing Company, Inc.,
New York

Library of Congress Catalog Number: 76-52317

ISBN: 0-525-08949-7

10   9   8   7   6   5   4   3   2   1

The Armalite 15 is quite probably the most lethal weapon of its type in the world today at ranges up to 500 yards impacting upon a thin-skinned animal i.e. man.

Due to the high muzzle velocity and boat-tailed bullet design, the bullet tumbles or yaws on impact. This, coupled with the fact that the projectile expends its total energy in a very short space, causes an immense build-up of hydrostatic pressure within any body containing fluid. The resultant wound cavity is enormous and there is a tremendous shock effect.

Description of the American Armalite 15 assault rifle issued by the distributors, Cooper-MacDonald, Inc.

One of the greatest problems liberalism faces is its desperate shortage of adherents who recognise the brutal reality of an illiberal world, and who know that it is not possible to preserve freedom and everything that goes with it unless the defenders are as hard, single-minded and, when it becomes necessary, ruthless as our enemies.

Bernard Levin in THE TIMES

Death of a
Thin-skinned Animal

The jungle was all around him.

The jungle is all around you wherever you are, his mother used to tell him when he was small. They were living in Ruislip then and he would look out of the window half-expecting a tiger to spring out of the sweet peas at the bottom of the garden.

He wished he were in Ruislip now. A childish wish, as childish as the tears he wept over Kirote, who had been dead since dawn and was beginning to smell.

Mechanically he brushed the flies away from the body with one hand and his own tears with the other. He wept partly from grief and partly from self-pity, but mostly from physical weakness. He had been underfed, overworked and sporadically maltreated for two years. Kirote was the only friend he made in that time. He had shared a cell with him and six other Africans – five thieves and a simple-minded rapist.

He would have liked to bury him, but there was no time for niceties. Leave him to the hyenas and vultures and whatever else scavenged that part of the rain-forest. He took the knife they had taken from the dead guard and, sniffing back his tears, moved on through the bush, following narrow paths and animal tracks, always heading west, taking a bearing from the sun whenever he glimpsed it through the perpetual gloom.

His feet were tender, his legs ached, he was thirsty. But he kept on at a rhythmic pace.

They had been in the rain-forest six days, living off wild bananas and forest snails and yams stolen from the occasional plantation. Now he was alone and frightened.

I

RICHARD ABBOTT stood at the north-east corner of Trafalgar Square in the dark and the falling rain, hesitating before the next step, which simply meant crossing the street to the all-night post office and sending a cable.

But it was like crossing the Rubicon, an act of war. So he hesitated (he who hesitates is lost, his mother would have instantly said). Yet it wasn't really hesitation, he told himself, more the moment of stillness before action, the deep breath before the high dive.

Two men went by discussing *Hamlet*, the classic of hesitation. But it had no relevance. After all, he wasn't going to kill his father. The thought made him smile, and a passing woman wondered if he was mad and quickened her pace.

The wind got up suddenly and he shivered, aware of a physical discomfort he had so far ignored.

Big Ben struck two and he shivered again and crossed the wet street to the post office. Edith Cavell's statue glistened in the rain. He had always meant to read a life of her.

Only one section of the post office was open. It was occupied by four counter-clerks, three of them reading, a tramp having a warm and an American matron with a large hat and metallic voice, seeking information.

He looked for the box containing telegram forms and couldn't find it. It irritated him. It must be there.

'Where's the box with telegram forms?' he said to one of the reading clerks, who pointed to another clerk and went back to his reading.

He repeated the question to the other clerk, who took a form from a drawer and gave it to him.

'Don't you usually keep them in a box this side of the counter?'

8

'We put out four thousand of 'em,' said the clerk. 'Know what happened? They went in three days. It's the women and kids. Take 'em by the handful. God knows what they do with 'em.'

He wrote the telex address at the top of the form, then wrote his brief message and stared at it.

'And this one,' said the metallic voice, 'is for Homer. That's my nephew, in Bethlehem, P.A. How long will it take?'

He caught a whiff of methylated spirits mixed with stale piss and sweat as the tramp shuffled and snuffled by.

'Would your honour spare a copper or two for a cup of tay? It's destroyed wid thirst I am, and that's a fact.'

'Bugger off.'

The tramp shuffled away without even looking at him.

Abbott handed the message to the clerk, who looked at the telex address.

'It's only round the corner,' said the clerk.

'I know where it is.'

'I mean, you could deliver it yourself. It wouldn't take five minutes.'

'I don't want to deliver it myself.'

The clerk gave up and started to count the words.

'You sure you got this right?' The clerk tried again.

'Yes.'

'It sounds funny.'

'It's meant to be,' said Abbott. 'It's a joke. To laugh at.'

Outside it was still raining. He walked up Charing Cross Road to Cambridge Circus and stared at the posters outside the Palace Theatre without seeing them.

He was hungry. He needed a shave. He needed a bath. Ah, the luxury of a bath. He took a deep breath, dreaming of a perfumed bath, and became aware of a familiar stench and a familiar Irish whine.

'Could yous be sparing a few pennies for a pour ould fella, yer honour. . . .'

The tramp still did not look at him, did not even realise he was begging from the same man.

Abbott was about to send him away again when an idea, or

the beginnings of an idea, occurred to him. He turned towards the tramp, who looked as evil as he smelt, held on to his rising stomach by an effort of will, and smiled.

'Sure now,' he said, in his best bog-Irish, 'I've a shilling or two to be sharing wid a dacent Irish lad.'

'It's Irish y'are yerself?' The tramp's voice was hoarse with delight.

'Irish as the pigs in Dublin.'

'Ye speak like a man from Cork, I'm thinking.'

Abbott nodded. 'Skibbereen,' he said.

'Ye don't say? I once had an aunt in Ballydehob at the top end o' Roaring Water Bay. A brave little place altogether. How much did ye say ye'd got?'

Abbott took out his loose change and several pound notes. 'Seventy-eight pence. And a bit of folding money.'

'Jesus Mary and Joseph, but that's a tidy sum.'

'And where d'ye suppose we'd be getting a drop of something to drink at this time o' night?'

'Ye've come to the very man, yer honour, the very man,' said the tramp, breaking wind with excitement.

2

FRANK SMITH heard a church bell ringing in the distance, gradually growing louder and more insistent and finally turning into the ringing of a telephone. He was dreaming. I am dreaming, he told himself, and woke up.

He lifted the receiver off the cradle, still not sure if he was in the dream.

'Hallo?'

'Frank?'

It was Fawley, Duty Officer at Holland Park, where the Department had its discreet offices.

'We've had a telex we can't make head nor tail of.'

'What do you mean?'

'We can't decode it. At least Jones can't – he's the cipher bod on duty. But it's not in the book.'

'Not in the book? It must be.'

For a moment Frank Smith wondered if he was back in the dream.

'Jones says we haven't used that code for two years.'

'Where's the message from?'

'The all-night post office by Trafalgar Square, timed three minutes past two.'

'Then it's obvious. Who's our man in Trafalgar Square?'

'Sorry?'

'It's a gag, don't you see? Young Ronnie Simmons or some other idiot. Out on the town. Two o'clock in the morning. Stoned out of their minds. Let's wake old Smithy up with a hot flash about the Gunpowder Plot or the Fall of Troy or something.'

There was a brief silence.

'Funny they should use a two-year-old code, though.'

'All right then, what's the problem? If it's not in the

current book it'll be in one of the old books. Or is Jones too bloody idle to dig them out?'

Then he remembered. The old code-books were in Archives, locked in the safe. And only section heads had the keys.

'Shit,' he said.

'What?'

'I'll be over.'

He put the phone down and lay back for a moment, listening to the rain on the window, thinking how warm and comfortable it was in bed and how he'd like to stay there, trying not to think about anything else – above all, trying not to think about Richard Abbott, but knowing all the time that that was who the message was from. He was the only agent in the field with an out-of-date code. Except that he wasn't supposed to be in the field. He was supposed to be dead.

He got up and reached for the carefully folded clothes on the chair by the window. He was a bachelor, a neat man and tidy in his ways, except when drunk or depressed.

He dressed rapidly, looking out of the window at the black night and falling rain, shaking his head and clicking his tongue to propitiate the unknown gods.

A waiting car whisked him through the wet black night to Holland Park, where the Department had its offices in a solidly handsome Georgian house standing well back from the road behind an ivy-clad wall. It had once been the offices of a firm of marine insurance brokers and according to a plate on the wall – if you could find it under all that ivy – it still was.

He showed his pass to the night janitor and went straight to his office.

Fawley was waiting for him and handed him the telex message, which had gone first to the Foreign Office, then by teleprinter to that L-shaped building behind Waterloo Station where Secret Intelligence Service has its not so secret headquarters. 'Sis', as they call it in the trade, relayed it to Holland Park.

Smith stared at the message with distaste, not wanting to know what it said.

'It won't be anything good, that's for sure,' he said gloomily.

He went down to Archives, woke up the Duty Officer, opened one of the safes and found the code-book he wanted. He signed for it and took it back to his office. Then he started to decode the message.

After he had written it out in clear he sat staring at it.

'It's from Abbott,' he said, as if that explained everything.

'Abbott?' said Fawley, 'I thought he was dead.'

'So did a lot of people.'

For a moment he wished that Abbott, his friend for fifteen years, was dead. The wish was not entirely selfish.

He picked up the phone, flashed the operator impatiently.

'Come on, come on!' At last he heard the sleepy voice.

'What the hell are you doing – having a kip?' The man started to make an excuse. 'Never mind the backchat, get me the Minister. No, make it the Controller.'

'He'll be in bed and asleep.'

'Then bloody well wake him up.'

He put the phone down, drummed his fingers on the desk, picked nervously at his nose and stared at Fawley, who pointed to the message.

'May I?'

'Help yourself.'

The message simply said: *Contract will be completed on or before the fourteenth.*

'Am I allowed to know what the contract was?'

'Why not? By tomorrow the whole department will know and, if we're unlucky enough, the whole bloody country.'

He let out a worried sigh, as if trying or hoping to diminish what he was about to say.

'Abbott's contract was to kill Colonel Njala.'

'Christ.'

'You may well call upon him, Fawley, we're going to need all the help we can get.'

The phone rang. It was the Controller, sleepy and bad-tempered.

'If it's anything less than a declaration of war. . . .'

Smith told him what it was.

'Oh my God.'

The Controller, who was sitting up in bed, suddenly felt weak and flopped back, waking up his wife, who grumbled unintelligibly and kicked him.

'Fat cow, what do you think you're doing?'

'Eh?' said Smith at the other end.

'I suppose it *is* Abbott? I mean, it's not a hoax?'

The hope in the Controller's voice was pitiful.

'The message had both his safety checks.'

'He must be out of his mind.'

'Doesn't make him any the less dangerous.'

The Controller gave a sigh like a groan.

'What a mess. Teach them to play at power politics. . . . Bloody politicians. All their bloody fault in the first bloody place. . . .' Another groaning sigh. 'Oh well, you'd better get the Minister. Get everybody – Ross of Special Branch – no, he's away. Make it Shepherd since he does all the work anyway. Whatsisname from MI5 or whatever they call it these days, and that chap from the Foreign Office – well, you know who to get. My office in half an hour. And see the bloody heating's on, will you?'

He put the phone down and dropped back heavily on the bed, getting another reflex kick from his wife, but he was too worried to react.

He pulled the bedclothes up over his head and buried his face in the pillow as he did when he was a boy trying to hide from the world.

After a few minutes he got up quietly and dressed without putting the light on. His wife started to snore.

While the Controller was dressing awkwardly in the dark and trying not to disturb his high-kicking wife, Smith was trying to find the Minister, who was not at his town house or his country house or the flat of his recognised mistress. A steeply superior private secretary, who had trouble keeping awake, hadn't the foggiest where his master might be. Smith kept his temper and persisted.

'What is all this, dear boy, a Red Alert?'

'An emergency.'

'What category of emergency, dear boy?'

Smith could hear him yawning. 'I don't know,' he said. 'What category would you put assassination in?'

'Assassination? Of my master?' He was awake now all right.

'Of someone a good deal more important than your bloody master.'

'Good God, who?'

'Ah,' said Smith, giving the classic security excuse, 'that's something you don't need to know . . . dear boy.'

The secretary, getting less superior by the minute, gave him the number of the radio telephone in the Minister's car. His master, he said, had gone out about midnight accompanied only by his bodyguard.

Smith got through to the bodyguard, an armed Special Branch man who was alone in the car, staring at the rain, outside a block of flats off the Fulham Road.

'I can't,' said the Special Branch man. 'He's busy. You know what I mean? *Busy.* Over.'

'I know what you mean and I know what his snotty little bastard of a secretary means. Now you get him – and quick. Over.'

'Christ, man, I can't just go and knock on the bloody door.'

'Then try throwing stones at the bloody window. But get him. Over and out.'

Smith hung up, then started to dial Joan Abbott's number, then hung up again. He didn't want to ring her. He felt sorry for her yet irritated by her. He had once fancied her and, after her divorce, took her out once or twice. But nothing came of it. He was too much of a bachelor and she was too neurotic. At least, that was the excuse he made to himself. But the truth was he felt guilty, not so much about her as about Abbott. Or rather, what he suspected the Department had done to Abbott. It was a suspicion he would only half admit, even to himself. But it was there, and at times it ached like an old wound. So he kept away from her. He had enough wounds. It was a reasonable, middle-aged, prudent attitude. And he despised it.

'She's so bloody neurotic,' he said complainingly. 'And half the time she's stoned.'

Fawley was about to say 'Who?' when he realised Smith was simply voicing his thoughts.

3

JOAN ABBOTT was standing by the window in the dark, looking down into the street, when the car drew up under a lamp-post. Another drew up behind it. Three men got out of the first car, two out of the second. She counted them. Twice. She'd been drinking and wanted to be sure.

They stared up at her window, and instinctively she started back, then realised they couldn't see her in the dark room.

After a moment they moved off into the shadows. To keep watch no doubt, just as Richard said they would.

She saw a match flare in the darkness as one of them lit a cigarette. It made her feel the need for a cigarette herself, and she moved away from the window and lit one, her hand beginning to shake a little. But she felt elated. She was actually doing something. It was the first time Richard had involved her in anything to do with his work. Perhaps it was a sign. . . . She didn't pursue the thought but she felt her heart, like her hand, beginning to shake.

She needed another drink to steady herself. She switched on the table-lamp and poured herself a whisky from the almost empty decanter, added a splash of soda and swallowed it down. That was better. That was much better. She poured herself another but added more soda. She wouldn't knock this one back like an oyster though; she would take her time over it. Sip it. Like a bloody lady.

It was very strange about Richard. She had thought he was dead. So had the Department. Even Frank Smith had thought so. Which somehow seemed to make it official. And then, the night before last, right out of the blue, just like that, he had telephoned : 'This is Richard.'

A voice from the dead. She had stammered and stuttered like a fool.

Would she help him? He'd just landed in England but didn't want anyone to know.

Not even Frank Smith and the Department? Especially Frank Smith and the Department.

It all seemed very mysterious, but she had learned a long time ago not to ask questions. Of course she knew he was an agent (all the wives knew; it was departmental policy). She even knew he had gone to Africa, because he'd told her he was going and asked her to look after some of his clothes.

The job had evidently gone wrong, because a few months later she read in the papers that he'd been arrested and jailed for spying in one of those new native republics with a new native name that no one can ever remember.

Of course, the papers didn't say Richard Abbott; they said some other name. But there was this photograph – and it was Richard all right.

And there was this big speech by the President, Colonel Mumbo-Jumbo or something, saying that God had appeared to him in a vision, telling him to expel all who held British passports, since the British were plotting his downfall and anyway were an evil thing in the sight of the Lord.

And she had been worried for Richard, jailed in that barbaric land where whole tribes had been wiped out at the whim of the God-inspired colonel. But Frank Smith had called round and told her the Government were trying to arrange a behind-the-scenes deal for Richard's release. But something must have gone wrong with that too because, though she waited months, she heard no more. And when she finally rang Frank Smith he said that God had appeared to the colonel in another vision, telling him not to release spies and other enemies of the State.

In the end she had given up hope – the hope that one day, despite their divorce, Richard would return to her.

Then, a few weeks ago, Frank Smith had called round again and told her Richard had broken out of jail, killing a guard and escaping into the jungle.

So there was still a chance he might make it back to England? Frank Smith shook his head, and flicked ash nervously over the carpet. If the colonel's police didn't get him, the jungle would. All the odds were against him.

'All the odds,' she repeated slowly – she was a little drunk at the time. 'And no doubt the Gods. Who are sods. To a man.'

She hiccuped and then giggled – from the same nervous compulsion that made Frank Smith flick ash over the carpet. They got solemnly drunk together and went solemnly to bed together. When she woke up in the morning she felt like a whore. And when he asked to see her again she refused because she thought he was asking out of politeness.

And now here she was getting drunk again – and Richard already back in the country. She must not drink any more. She must keep a clear head. The thought depressed her, and a feeling of middle-aged loneliness went through her like a cold wind. And she felt like a drink again. She always felt like a drink when she was sad. Or when she was happy. She had to admit it though, she was drinking too much these days. Still, as long as nobody knew.

Frank Smith said to Fawley as he dialled her number : 'Let's hope she's not stoned.'

'At this time of night? Surely she'll be in bed and asleep?'

'When Special Branch rang through they said there was a light in the flat. Which means she's up. And if she's up she's drinking.'

'I only met her once,' said Fawley. 'I thought she was nice.'

'She is. But sad. One of the sad.'

He knew it was her before she spoke. She had a habit of lifting the receiver, then hesitating before she spoke, as if she were afraid of bad news or human contact or anything else that might hurt.

'Hallo?'

'Joan? Frank Smith. Did I get you out of bed?'

'No. I couldn't sleep, so I got up and had a drink. . . .' She hesitated. 'I thought it might make me sleepy.'

She stifled a hiccup.

'Joan, we think Richard's back in England.'

'Really?' She hoped she sounded surprised.

'He hasn't been in touch with you?'

'Nobody's been in touch with me. Nobody ever is. I don't count any more.'

The note of self-pity and reproach was a sure sign that she was drunk. He felt guilty nevertheless.

'Joan, look, I wanted to get in touch with you, but . . . well, the last time. . . . I mean, you told me not to, didn't you?'

'I am not blaming anyone,' she said with a dignity that was only slightly diminished by another hiccup.

He realised he was getting away from the point; but conversations with Joan always got away from the point, if they ever had one.

'Joan, if Richard gets in touch, will you let me know immediately? It's very important.'

'You said he'd never make it, didn't you? You said it wasn't possible.'

'Then I was wrong,' said Smith patiently.

'What's so important? I mean, why do you want him?'

'Well. . . . I can't actually discuss it, Joan. It's a security matter.'

He waited for her to say something, but she kept silent.

'Joan, are you still there?'

Still no answer.

'Joan? Joan?'

'Frank, who are those men outside disguised as policemen?'

Smith put his hand over the mouthpiece. 'Stoned,' he said to Fawley, 'but not stupid.'

Then to Joan : 'Ah. I was going to explain about them. They're, er, from Special Branch.'

'You must want him badly. What *has* he done?'

'Well . . . nothing. It's what he might do.'

'Might do? You mean he's mad or something?'

'No, I don't mean he's mad. Look, Joan, I can't explain; it's – it's classified information. But, if he gets in touch with you, let me know. Honestly, Joan, it's for his own good.'

He didn't sound very convincing and he knew it. Again there was no answer from the other end.

'You do believe me, don't you? Joan?'

'I believe you.'

'Another thing. The Special Branch chaps will want to . . . take a look round the flat. If you don't mind.'

'Would it make any difference if I did?'

'It's just a matter of routine. You know what policemen are like,' he added feebly.

'No,' she said. 'I don't.'

'Well—'

'They think Richard's hiding here. Is that it?'

'It's simply a possibility they have to exclude.'

'And then I'll be – what's the phrase? Eliminated from their inquiries?'

'Can I tell them it's all right?'

'You can tell them to get a move on. I want to get back to bed.'

There was a click as she hung up.

'She started off stoned,' said Smith, 'but all the time she was sobering up – and getting smarter with it.'

'You think she knows something – about Abbott?'

'I don't know. She's a . . . confusing sort of person. Neurotics always are.'

The two Special Branch men searched the flat quickly and efficiently. They were polite and apologised for disturbing her when she saw them out. They both had the same kind of flat wary face – or perhaps it was just the expression that was the same – and big feet. They really did have big feet. It surprised her.

She went into the sitting-room and pulled the curtain halfway across the window. That was to be the signal to Richard that the flat had been searched and was now clear. Then she poured herself another drink. She felt she deserved it.

They were hiding beside a dirt road to let a platoon of drunken soldiers pass when it happened. The dirt road led to a village, where the soldiers had been questioning the people about the two fugitives from the prison. The people could tell them nothing because they had nothing to tell. This made the soldiers angry and they bayoneted the headman, raped the only two women who had not had time to hide, and got drunk on maize beer.

They marched off along the dirt road singing. The sergeant leading the platoon saw a grey parrot in the undergrowth by the side of the road and started firing at it. Then the other soldiers started firing. The parrot flew away unharmed and screeching. The soldiers laughed and emptied their carbines into the undergrowth regardless. Then they marched on, in ragged formation and out of step like a bunch of black clowns.

One of the random bullets hit Kirotè in the belly. That's how it happened. They couldn't hit the parrot, they couldn't hit a horse if they were holding it by the stirrup, they couldn't hit anything as long as they were aiming at it. But they hit Kirote. They hit him all right.

'We shouldn't have hidden,' Abbott said. 'We should've let them take aim at us. Then they'd have hit the parrot.'

He carried Kirote to a stream, washed the wound and examined it.

'You need help,' he said. 'I'll go to the village.'

'No,' said Kirote in the basic English Abbott had taught him. 'They frightened. Send for soldiers. That way two die. This way one die.'

'You're not going to die,' he said, trying to sound as if he meant it.

Kirote shook his head. 'Die before sun-up,' he said without emotion.

And he did. Abbott held him in his arms all night, trying to keep him warm. He also tried to stay awake but must have dozed off before dawn. He was woken up by the coldness of the dead body.

4

LIKE a number of other people that night Alice Campbell was woken up by a call from Frank Smith. He told her briefly about Abbott and asked if she could be at the Controller's office in half an hour.

She said yes, as he knew she would, which was why he had rung her. His own secretary, who was an admiral's daughter and was weekending with her latest man, would have sworn like a three-badge stoker if he'd rung her at that hour. And the other senior secretaries were either married or living out of town. So Alice was the natural choice. He knew she'd be alone; she always was.

She was a plain, quiet girl with a squint, which made her keep her head down to avoid meeting people's eyes. It gave her a shy, slightly coy look. She had a good figure though, and Smith sometimes felt a twinge of desire when he passed her in a corridor or watched her cross the canteen balancing a tray.

She was nearly thirty, but Smith always thought of her as a girl. There was something irremediably spinsterish about her.

She usually fell in love with the men she worked for, though they never knew it. She showed her love by looking after them in small ways, covering up for them, being generally efficient and thoughtful, and occasionally presenting them with small pots of home-made jam. They took her care and efficiency for granted, gave away the pots of jam and never noticed her.

Abbott was the exception. Abbott noticed her. She had been seconded to him (the Department, which was run on para-military lines, favoured words like seconded) when he did a desk job for a few months before going to Africa. His marriage had broken up, he was at a loose end and he took her (and not only her) out to dinner a few times. At that time he had no intention of sleeping with her. Their relationship was pleasant and uncomplicated, and he wanted to keep it like that. He knew some of the men in the Department slept with their secretaries, or other people's secretaries, but he never had – less from principle than laçk of opportunity. As an agent in the field he spent most of his time abroad.

For her part Alice was in love with him as she usually was with her current boss, though the love had never been consciously sexual before. This time it was different – perhaps because Abbott had taken notice of her, had actually taken her out, talked to her, treated her like a woman instead of a piece of office furniture. Not that his attitude was ever less than what her mother called correct. Her feelings, on the other hand, were getting less correct all the time. She noticed his hands and wondered what it would be like to be touched by them. They were warm, dry, long-fingered and lively-looking. The thought of their touching her aroused her – uncomfortably at times. She tried to repress it, but the thought kept coming back at awkward moments when she was off guard – in the office, in the canteen, going upstairs, when she was supposed to be listening to what someone else was saying.

Then he disappeared for a week. He told her he was going to a conference. She noticed that Frank Smith and the Controller were away at the same time, no doubt attending the same conference at one of the Department's country houses. When he returned he was withdrawn and restless, and she was sure he had lost what little interest he'd had in her. He didn't seem to notice her any more.

Alice was overtaken by a quiet despair. Whenever a man got interested in her – and that was rare enough – something went wrong. Or if nothing went wrong he simply got tired of her. Only two of her relationships developed past the petting stage. And then the two men left her as soon as they had slept with her, having achieved their simple objective.

If you sleep with men they get tired of you in the end, her mother used to tell her. And if you don't they get tired of you in the beginning, she wanted to reply, but never did. Her mother, a widow living in Beckenham, would have been shocked. As it was she didn't approve of her daughter living alone in a flat in Notting Hill Gate, which she thought was little better than Soho, – the Square Mile of Vice, as her favourite tabloid called it.

So it seemed part of a familiar, perhaps inevitable pattern that Richard Abbott should lose interest in her. Everyone else had.

Then one day when she'd finally given up hope, he broke off while dictating some typically cryptic inter-office memo and asked her out to dinner, barely waiting for her reply before going on with the memo.

They went to an Italian restaurant in Kensington Church Street as usual, shook hands with Vittorio as usual and sat at their usual table upstairs. Nothing else about the evening was usual though. Abbott hardly said a word during the meal, and drank steadily. When they had finished the first bottle of Chianti he ordered a second.

After the meal he said, 'Let's have coffee at my place.'

She had never had coffee at his place. She had never even been to his place. They had always had coffee at her place. It was the custom, and she was filled with dark forebodings, like a heroine about to be raped. She was also filled with curiosity.

In the taxi back to his place he held her hand tightly. He had never done anything like that before, and it thrilled her to the centre of her loins.

His place was an Edwardian mansion flat off the Bayswater Road. Big and spacious and untidy, books on the floor and on tables, clothes over the backs of chairs, and almost nothing in its place. Tall windows overlooked a quiet square on one side, a quiet street on the other. Both the street and the square had plane trees.

It was getting dark, and they stood by one of the tall windows looking down at the plane trees in the quiet square. Alice thought they looked old and sad in the orange light of the sodium lamps.

She sneaked a sidelong glance at Abbott. He was staring

down into the square, not moving, hardly breathing it seemed. There was something animal-like in his stillness and it made her nervous.

'What about coffee?' she said, her words seeming to echo in the big half-dark room.

He turned and took her in his arms. The abruptness of it startled her and she struggled for a moment, then relaxed and clung to him.

After a while he took her into the bedroom, which also overlooked the quiet square, and they undressed in the twilight. She kept her eyes lowered, partly from habit, partly from modesty, but she knew he was looking at her. She also knew she had a good figure and was blushing with pleasure.

In bed she surprised him with her warmth and loving and a kind of female sensuality that is almost beyond sensuality, and anyway beyond words. For some reason he had expected her to be awkward and inhibited.

As for her, she thought everything about him was wonderful because she was in love and therefore in heaven and in heaven you can do no wrong.

'Isn't this lovely?' she said, happily lost in a mix of slippery limbs and sliding bodies.

Later he got up and made sweet black coffee laced with rum, which they drank by the light of the bedside lamp.

Then she laid her head on his chest and thought of nothing, enjoying the warmth and closeness of him, while he stared at the ceiling.

Then they made love again, sometimes smiling at each other. Time stood still, and eventually they fell asleep in each other's arms.

She got up soon after five and dressed by the oyster light of dawn, watching him as he slept. Then she tiptoed round the flat, her shoes in her hand, absorbing the atmosphere, taking in details, remembering the man she had slept with. She was happier in those few minutes than she'd ever been before or perhaps would ever be again.

She went back to the bedroom, brushed her lips across his forehead. He stirred, murmured something unintelligible and slept on. She stood smiling down at him, then put on her shoes and let herself out into streets that were wet with early-morning rain.

She picked up a cab in the Bayswater Road, her head full of practical plans, which she elaborated on the way to her flat. To feed the canary, have a bath, have breakfast, do some washing, do some shopping. Above all, to choose the right dress, so that she would look nice for him when he came to the office that morning.

But he did not come to the office that morning or any other morning. At first she thought he'd gone off to one of those mysterious conferences. Nevertheless, she felt cheated in some way, almost betrayed, because he had said nothing to her about it. Come to think of it, he had said remarkably little to her about anything.

All day in the office she waited for him to ring, and all evening in her flat she sat by the phone and leapt like a salmon when it did actually ring. It was her mother in Beckenham, ringing for a cosy chat. She got rid of her with an implausible excuse and a promise to ring back the next day. And sat by the phone and waited. And waited. It didn't ring again.

She followed the same routine for the next two days, then rang Abbott's flat. No answer. At the end of the week, she went round there, knocked on the door. No answer. Knocked louder. Still no answer. The whole place sounded empty and hollow. The curtains were drawn as if somebody had just died.

And somebody has, she thought. Me. Little old me.

Later she heard from Frank Smith that Abbott had gone to West Africa. Then, two or three months later, came the report that he'd been arrested for spying. She had wondered what his mission was, but that was the kind of question you didn't ask in the Department. Anyway, if you waited long enough you usually got the answer.

She'd waited two years, and now she'd got the answer. Two long years. Some years are longer than others, of course. These two years had been very long. And very lonely. At first she thought about him constantly but as time passed she thought about him less and it hurt less, though even when she wasn't thinking about him she was aware of a dull ache never too far away. In the end even that stopped, and all she was left with was a sort of dead area round the heart. A feeling of slight numbness, not unpleasant.

Now, after one phone call, it had come suddenly and painfully alive again. She felt angry and bitter. I hate him, she thought as she dressed hurriedly in the tiny bathroom of her flat.

She heard the mini-cab she had ordered pulling up outside and went down and let herself out into the cold night and the still-falling rain.

5

IN LITTLE MORE than half an hour everyone was at the Controller's office except the Minister. There was Armstrong, Permanent Under Secretary at the Foreign Office; Blake, an effeminate-looking liaison officer from SIS headquarters; Chief Superintendent Shepherd of Special Branch; Brigadier Buckley of what used to be MI5; and of course Alice, Frank Smith and the Controller.

Alice had already made coffee, and the Controller was lacing it with a cheap and fiery brandy someone gave him for Christmas and which he'd been trying to get rid of ever since. He hated waste. Frank Smith was handing round the sugar.

The office was large and comfortable but not yet warm, and everyone was glad of the coffee and brandy, which stopped a tendency to shiver.

'It must be all of ten weeks since he escaped,' said Armstrong. 'What's he been doing in the meantime?'

'Surviving, presumably,' said Blake.

Silly bloody answer, Armstrong thought, and typical of Sis. If he hadn't survived he'd hardly be back in England sending barmy bloody messages in the middle of the night.

Armstrong distrusted all Intelligence people. They spent money and caused trouble. Well, now the trouble was coming home to roost. He almost smiled. He enjoyed seeing other people in the kaka, as he classically called it.

'And not a word from him till now?' said Brigadier Buckley.

'That's why we thought he was dead,' said the Controller.

'I know that part of the world,' said Blake, 'and it must have taken him at least a week to get through the jungle. Probably nearer two when you think he'd have to hide a good deal of the time.'

Buckley said: 'And he couldn't have been in much shape after a couple of years in one of Njala's bug-infested jails. I hear they can be quite rough on the inmates.'

Blake nodded. 'As rough as the Russians. But not quite so sophisticated. Did he make it alone?'

'He escaped with another man, a black man, from what we've heard,' said the Controller. 'But the black man got killed. Some natives found his body near their village.'

'And Abbott?'

The Controller shrugged. 'Another body was found a few miles away, in a river. The body of a white man, half-eaten by crocodiles and quite unrecognisable. Njala's police apparently found something on the body that made them assume it was Abbott.'

'Sounds as if Abbott found the body first,' said Buckley.

'He must be quite a chap,' said Blake.

'He is,' said Frank Smith suddenly. 'Quite a chap. Sugar, Mr Blake?'

'Where the hell's the Minister?' said the Controller.

'Having trouble getting out of a warm bed, I imagine,' said Armstrong.

There were one or two knowing smiles. The Minister's sexual diversions were a common source of gossip and amusement among those who considered themselves *cognoscenti*.

'Do we know who the latest is?' someone asked.

'My spies tell me,' said Armstrong, heavily facetious, 'that it's a long-legged black girl with a movement like a Swiss watch.'

'And,' said Blake, who hated to be outdone over inside gossip, 'with oral proclivities.'

The laughter that greeted this assured him he hadn't been outdone by Armstrong, which made him deeply happy.

Alice kept her head lowered and sharpened a pencil to unnecessary fineness.

One of those who didn't laugh was Chief Superintendent Shepherd, who was staring stolidly out of the window at the black night, busy with his own thoughts.

Twats, he was thinking, upper-class twats. Wasting time

giggling and gossiping like a bunch of girls when there was a killer on the loose. He had little time for Intelligence people, whom he considered overpaid, overbearing and oversexed. He felt similarly about politicians and higher civil servants. He only really liked other policemen. In fact, he wasn't very bright – except at his job, which largely consisted of bullying information out of people.

'What do you think of Abbott?' Buckley asked him.

'I think he's mad.'

'You would,' said Smith with another of his sudden interventions.

'He's entitled to be after what he's been through,' said the Controller mildly, giving Smith a look that said : Cool it.

Smith disliked policemen of all kinds.

At that point the Minister arrived in his opera cloak – not that anyone believed he'd been to the opera.

'Sorry I'm late,' he said smoothly, 'but I had difficulty getting away from a party.'

'Otherwise known as the party of the second part,' someone said in a stage whisper that would have reached the upper circle.

The Minister was middle-aged and stocky, not the figure for a cloak, but he had carried off less likely things. He had the face of a professional politician, ready to smile and giving nothing away. He was a miner's son and boasted of it, but the only time he had been down the pits was on a tour of inspection when he became an MP. He was a bright scholarship boy who had gone far and would go farther. But he had taken care not to lose his Yorkshire accent altogether; it allowed him to speak as a man of the people. He could also turn on a bluff Yorkshire manner when it suited him.

Now he was at his smoothest with hardly a trace of provincial accent or mannerism.

'Coffee and brandy for the Minister, Alice,' the Controller said.

'Just brandy, thank you.'

'It's not very good, I'm afraid. And I've no soda.'

'I don't take soda.'

He took a gulp of the brandy and put the glass down.

'Where did you get it?'

'A friend.'

'A friend?' said the Minister. 'I think I'll take coffee with it after all.'

When Alice gave him the coffee he poured the rest of the brandy in it and drank it down quickly.

'No thank you,' he said as Alice was about to pour him another. He smiled at her.

'I needed that,' he said.

She looked at him curiously. He was what her mother would call a roué. But a working-class roué seemed a contradiction in terms. Roués, she felt, should be upper class and effete. Chinless wonders with wet lips and an inability to pronounce their rs.

'Now,' said the Minister, 'what's all this about an assassination attempt?'

'Ah, well . . .' the Controller began.

'I tell you frankly I found it both shocking and incredible. Am I really to believe that the British Government actually planned the assassination in the first place? Assassination? Of a black man?'

His tone seemed to imply that it might have been less heinous had it merely been a white man.

'I mean, assassination's not our thing, as they say. Is it?'

The Controller waited, not sure whether the question was rhetorical and the Minister about to launch into one of his well-known political harangues.

'Is it?' the Minister repeated.

The Controller, who could be as smooth as the Minister, said : 'Of course it isn't, Minister. Of course it isn't. Not as a rule, that is. . . . Er, don't take any of this, Alice.'

Alice put her pencil and notebook down.

'But occasionally, Minister – very occasionally, one is happy to say – for reasons of high policy and international welfare and even for the maintenance of peace, it becomes imperative to . . . well, remove an enemy.'

'But this chap's a friend. A very good friend.'

'Ah,' said the Controller. 'Is a friend. Is. But two years ago. . . .'

He nodded to Armstrong, who said: 'It looked like war. Another Congo, another Biafra – but potentially far worse.'

'In what way?'

'It would've put our entire financial position there in jeopardy. We had a lot of money tied up there.'

'Ah,' said the Minister and nodded. He had a deep understanding of the importance of money.

'On top of that,' Armstrong went on, 'it would've let the Russians in – in a big way. Apart from the loss of life. Mostly to the natives, of course.'

'Well, there's always a silver lining,' said the Minister, who had a taste for irony. 'But where does Njala come in?'

'He was threatening to start it.'

'A war? All on his own?'

'With Russian backing. And that could've brought the Americans in. And God knows what *that* might have escalated into.'

'The situation really was rather fraught,' said the Controller. 'That's why such a . . . such an extreme course of action was decided on.'

'Decided by whom?' The Minister almost snapped the question.

'By your office, Minister.' The reply came as smooth as velvet.

'I wasn't *in* office two years ago.'

'Ah,' said the Controller, 'then it must've been – let's see, it was just before the last reshuffle but one. In which case—'

'Oh never mind,' said the Minister. 'It would have come through Cabinet anyway. So you sent an agent?'

'Richard Abbott. Best man we had.'

'Who failed.'

'Who was betrayed.' Smith intervened again.

'By whom?'

34

'By one of his local contacts presumably,' said the Controller.

'I don't believe that,' said Smith flatly.

The Controller concealed his annoyance. 'It's the obvious explanation. In fact, the only explanation.'

'Do you have another explanation?' The Minister addressed Smith directly.

'I have no explanation at all,' said Smith. 'But something smells.'

He hesitated. The Controller's face was as blank as a sheet of glass, but Smith knew he was annoyed.

'Well, go on,' said the Minister.

'The only two local contacts Abbott had were two natives I recruited myself more than ten years ago – when I was attached to the British Consulate there. It was about the time we gave the country its independence.'

'Where was Njala at that time?' said the Minister.

'In jail,' said Smith. 'Where he should have stayed. Anyway, we thought we'd better have someone there to . . . keep an eye on things for us. And I recruited a couple of chaps who didn't like the new régime and who, I thought, would stay loyal to us.'

'Perhaps you thought wrong,' said the Minister.

Smith shrugged. 'They stayed loyal for ten years.'

'They might've talked to someone else they thought they could trust,' said the Controller. 'These things happen.'

'They didn't happen for ten years,' said Smith.

'But you have no alternative explanation?'

Oh yes, I have, thought Smith, but I'm not letting it loose in this company.

'No, Minister,' he said, 'I'm afraid I haven't.'

'Anyway, these local men weren't told the object of Abbott's mission, surely?'

'No,' said the Controller, 'but they knew he was a British agent. And that was enough.'

'And what happened to them? Do we know?'

'They were beaten to death by Njala's police,' said Smith. 'A funny kind of reward if they did betray Abbott.' He looked at the Controller. 'I think the whole thing stinks.'

'Anyway, all this is conjecture and doesn't really matter,' said the Controller. 'The only thing that matters now is stopping Abbott.'

'Do you think he's mad?' said the Minister.

He looked at Smith, who shrugged.

'I doubt it.'

'He must be,' said Chief Superintendent Shepherd. 'Only a madman would tell you in advance he was going to commit a murder.'

'He wouldn't see it as a murder,' said Smith. 'He'd see it as an execution. Ordered, after all, by us.'

'Yeah,' said Shepherd, 'madmen always see things a bit different from us, don't they?'

'Why *did* we change our minds about Njala?' said the Minister. 'And so suddenly. Remember, I wasn't in office at the time.'

'Ah well, there were a number of reasons,' began the Controller.

'Oil,' said Smith.

'There were other reasons too—'

'Uranium,' said Smith.

'Of course, of course,' said the Minister, 'that's why he's here now – to renegotiate his royalties.'

'I really must make the point that there *were* other considerations,' said the Controller.

'Quite, quite,' said the Minister, who couldn't care less about other considerations. 'Anyway, it should be relatively simple to stop him, shouldn't it? Abbott, I mean.'

There was a brief silence. Everyone stared at him. Then Smith spoke.

'He's worked for the Department for fifteen years; he knows exactly what we'll do to protect Njala and how we'll go about it. And he won't give a damn about his own life. He'll be about as easy to stop as a Kamikaze pilot.'

'Come now,' said the Minister, 'it *is* one man we're talking about, not an army.'

'An army might be easier,' said Smith. 'At least it'd be visible.'

'I think we've got a good chance of stopping him,' said Shepherd.

'A good *chance?*' said the Minister. 'Let's get this clear. It has to be a certainty. There can be no question of taking a chance with Njala's life. He's not some Dutch businessman, he's a visiting head of state.'

Another brief silence.

'Then put him on the next plane home,' the Controller said.

'Impossible. The negotiations will take a week, then the documents have to be drawn up and agreed. And Njala's not a man you can hurry.'

The Controller shrugged. He had made his point.

'We'll do our best to look after him.'

'I'm not interested in your best, only in protecting Njala – whatever it costs in men and money. So protect him. Completely.'

He paused for effect, looked around.

'Or you'll be out. All of you. I'll see to that.'

The moment he said it he knew he'd gone too far. He was talking like an amateur and the professionals merely looked at him blank-faced. He gave them one of his little-boy-lost sighs, took the sharpness out of his voice and let a note of Yorkshire homeliness creep in.

'I take that back,' he said. 'I'm rattled. I know I shouldn't be. But I am. This whole business, it's like a bloody nightmare. Sorry, gentlemen.'

He nearly said lads but caught himself in time. That would be overdoing it. However, the frank admission, the touch of Yorkshire bluffness, evoked one or two sympathetic smiles, and the Minister relaxed.

'Now, at the moment Njala is concerned primarily with his Swiss bank account – he's a great believer in rainy days – which makes him a relatively safe bet. I say relatively because in the end one can never be quite sure which way a nig-nog's going to jump, especially this one.'

He smiled when he said nig-nog, a daring word for a professed socialist and government minister to use these days, but he felt no uneasiness in company he regarded as reactionary. He thought it might tickle them. Their lack of response made him wonder if he had misjudged them again. He broadened his smile to cover the lapse.

'Now,' he said briskly, 'What immediate precautions are we taking for the safety of our honoured guest? Remember he had tea with the Queen yesterday, dinner with the PM last night. Be a terrible let-down to get murdered tomorrow. And don't say everything goes in threes.'

This brought a better response, and the Minister began to relax again.

'Well,' said the Controller, 'with Special Branch and D11 I've set up a joint security operation – with the specific object of stopping Abbott, of course.'

The Minister hesitated, then said: 'Stopping him? What does that mean?'

'Stopping him dead,' said the Controller flatly.

The Minister looked out of the window as if he had not heard the answer, knowing he should never have asked the question. There are things it is better for a Minister of the Crown not to know. Then he can be officially surprised about them afterwards, when the damage has fortunately been done.

The Controller saw his embarrassment and quickly started on the precautions taken – extra men posted at Njala's hotel, surveillance of the homes of Abbott's friends and relatives, a full description and photo of Abbott telexed to all police stations in London and the Home Counties with instructions to arrest and detain.

But the Minister barely listened. He felt he'd done his bit – chaired an emergency meeting in the middle of the night, encouraged, exhorted, threatened. In other words talked, which is as much as can reasonably be expected of a politician. Now all he wanted to do was get back to that flat off the Fulham Road and bury himself between a pair of black thighs.

Alice wasn't listening either. She was thinking about Abbott. So they were going to kill him. Well, it was his own fault, he'd brought it on his own head. Anyway, she didn't care any more, she told herself – even though her heart did beat painfully for a moment when she heard he was back in England. No, she didn't care. . . . Still, it gave her a strange feeling to sit there listening to plans to kill a man she'd once loved and slept with. All that warmth and vigour smashed into oblivion by a bullet. She tried, as she had tried before, to remember the night she spent with him. But she could only remember bits of it. His hands touching her, his mouth, his tongue, the throbbing in her loins. She couldn't remember what she wanted to remember most – the sensation of him inside her. She could imagine it but she couldn't remember it. At the time she thought she'd never forget it.

The Minister's voice cut across her thoughts.

'What's he like?'

Shepherd picked up a copy of the telexed description

'Five foot ten, dark hair, fresh complexion. . . .'

'As a man,' said the Minister wearily, 'as a man.'

There was a pause, then Smith spoke.

'Rather nice, actually.'

6

THE three men sitting in a car outside Joan Abbott's flat, two Special Branch men and a temporary detective constable co-opted from the local nick, were bored. At least the Special Branch men were. The TDC was simply taking his cue from them. If they were bored, he was bored. If they yawned, he yawned.

'He won't come here,' the Special Branch inspector said. 'He can't be that stupid.'

His sergeant nodded agreement. 'He must know the place'll be watched.'

The TDC opened his mouth to say something but changed his mind and pretended to stifle another yawn. Better to keep your mouth shut in front of the big boys unless you'd got something to say.

There was a noise farther down the street and some singing.

'What's all this?' said the inspector.

It was the TDC's moment.

'Meths drinkers from the building site by the canal,' he said. 'And they've had a skinful by the sound of it.'

By now they could make out five tramp-like figures approaching unsteadily, still singing.

'Christ,' said the inspector, 'meths-drinking bloody tramps. It's all we need.'

The five stopped under a street-lamp near the entrance to the flats. They were swaying like mandarins and seemed to be arguing.

'Ever seen a filthier-looking lot?' said the inspector.

Suddenly a fight broke out. The two other Special Branch men, who were watching the back of the flats, ran round to the front when they heard the noise. The inspector and the sergeant jumped out of their car.

40

'You stay here and keep an eye on the flats,' the inspector said to the TDC.

Three of the tramps ran off when they saw the Special Branch men. Only the two who were fighting remained.

'What the bloody hell d'you think you're up to?' said the inspector, shoving them apart.

One of the tramps turned to him and the inspector involuntarily stepped back as he caught a blast of evil-smelling breath.

'This big-mouthed fucker started it.'

'Who're you calling a—'

'Shut up,' the inspector shouted. 'And get out of here before I nick the pair of you. Go on now – move.'

The tramps moved.

The inspector and sergeant went back to the car, the other two to their posts at the back of the flats.

'Well, son,' said the inspector as he got into the car, 'anything to report?'

'Not really, sir,' said the TDC. 'Except that when they split up I noticed that one of the tramps ran round the back of the flats.'

'And why d'you think he did that?'

'Well, there's an alleyway at the back that's a short cut to the next street.'

'So it's the most sensible way to run.'

'I was just reporting,' said the TDC, 'like you said.'

'And a very good report too, son. Thank you very much.'

The TDC had an uncomfortable feeling that the inspector thought he was thick.

The inspector picked up the car's radio telephone, gave his call-sign and said, 'Nothing to report.'

But there was – or there might have been if he'd paid more attention to what the temporary detective constable had reported.

Joan Abbott woke up with a start. Someone was tapping at the back door, quietly but insistently. She got up, grabbed a dressing-gown and went into the kitchen, remembering in time not to switch the light on. The tapping had stopped. She listened, her heart thumping with excitement and fear. Then it started again. She went close to the door, which gave on to the fire-escape. Through the heavy fluted-glass panel she could make out the silhouette of a man, bulking against the night sky.

'Who is it?' she said in a low uncertain voice.

'Joan, it's me.'

She unlocked the door and let him in.

'Richard. . . .'

She stepped towards him.

'Don't get too near, I stink like a sewer. And I'm filthy dirty.'

'You want a bath?'

It sounded silly, but she didn't know what else to say.

'I'll put the immersion on,' she added.

'But no lights, remember.'

'I need a drink. What about you?'

'All right.'

'Whisky?'

'Fine.'

Really he would have preferred a nice cup of tea, but he didn't like to ask. He could tell she'd been drinking.

So they sat in the kitchen in the dark and drank whisky.

'What's it all about, Richard?'

'Didn't Frank Smith tell you?'

'No. He said the Department wanted to get hold of you and that it was urgent. I asked if you'd done anything, and he said it's what you might do.'

'Yes, well. . . .' He hesitated. 'It's better that you don't know too much.'

'Is it dangerous?'

'I'll be all right.'

'That's not what I asked.'

'Yes, it's dangerous.'

She didn't pursue the question. She had her own problems of survival. But she was glad to see him. He had an enduring quality, a stability she needed.

She drained her glass. The whisky and his presence made her feel better, especially the whisky.

'Another one?'

'I haven't finished this.'

She poured herself another large one, added a little water from the tap.

'How did you get past them, the police?'

'They were looking for one man on his own. I picked up with some tramps, bought them some booze and got them to kick up a bit of a shindig outside while I slipped round the back.'

'That was clever.'

'No. Instinct, training. I know how their minds work — their rigid thinking, their little rituals.' He smiled. 'Every hunt has its ritual. Like sex.'

Yes, sex, she thought. If only we could revive that little ritual. But the breakdown had lasted too long, and past a certain point these things were irreversible.

'I've made up a bed for you in the spare room,' she said. She would have liked to add: 'Or there's always mine.' But she didn't have the nerve.

They continued drinking in silence for a while, then Joan ran a bath and sorted out pyjamas and dressing-gown from the clothes he had left with her before he went to Africa.

Ah, that bath. The first proper bath he'd had for more than two years. It was strange but wonderfully soothing lying there in the dark, smelling the perfumed foamy water, feeling it slide over him like a caress. He stayed there till the water grew cold.

Afterwards he went into the kitchen and found Joan slumped across the table asleep.

He picked her up and carried her into her bedroom, laying her gently on the bed. As he did so she muttered something.

'What?'

'Or there's always mine,' she said.

Dreaming again. He covered her up and went out quietly.

The emergency meeting in Holland Park had broken up, leaving the Controller, Frank Smith and Chief Superintendent Shepherd to settle security details. The Controller thought the simplest plan would be to move Njala to one of the Department's safe houses, where conditions could be strictly controlled. The hotel was too exposed, too easy to find and impossible to make secure. But the house could be turned into a virtual fortress. 'And first of all, Abbott has to find it. Which could be quite a problem.'

'He's solved harder problems than that,' said Smith. 'A lot harder. Anyway, he must have thought about it.'

'Are you saying he knows we'll move Njala out of that hotel?'

'I'm saying he must have thought about it.'

'Unless I'm right – and he is mad.'

Shepherd was an obstinate man. Once he had got hold of an idea he hated to let go of it.

Smith studied him. He had small slate-coloured eyes set in a fleshy face and hair cropped so close that his head looked as if it had been worked on with a chisel. It also looked too small for his body. There was no visible neck, just a fold in the flesh between head and shoulders. Old Chisel Head, thought Smith, ignorant and obstinate.

'There's another aspect we haven't considered,' he said. 'Suppose Njala doesn't want to move?'

'Then we'll persuade him.'

'From what I've heard you might have to move the chorus-line of the Cabaret Club with him.'

'Like that, is he?' said Shepherd.

'Yes,' said the Controller, 'only more so. Well, if he wants girls he can have girls – as long as he gets out of that hotel.'

'But is it worth all the trouble?' said Smith. 'I mean, maybe he's safer where he is.'

'In a hotel that half London uses as a meeting-place?' said Shepherd. 'Where the foyer's busier than a main-line station, where anybody can walk in and out, use the cloakrooms, the bars, the tea-room, the public phones . . .'

'And where there are four entrances, to my knowledge,' said

the Controller, 'apart from staff and service entrances plus, I believe, a loading bay.'

'I've got men all over the place,' said Shepherd, 'but they can only keep their eyes open and hope. I mean, we can't control conditions there. We can't stop people and question them. It's a hotel. They've got a right to walk in and out. And Abbott could walk in with them. And we might never even notice – till it was too late.'

'Now wait a minute,' said Smith. 'He's not Black September or the Japanese Red Army. He's not going to mow down thirty people in the foyer with a submachine-gun just to get at Njala.'

'No?' said Shepherd.

'No.'

'You can guarantee that?'

'Yes.'

'Ballocks,' said Shepherd, 'you can't guarantee anything.'

'He's been a friend of mine for fifteen years. I know him.'

'After a couple of years in one of Njala's hell-holes I doubt if anyone knows him. I doubt if he even knows himself.'

'I know one thing: he never does anything without a reason.'

'Maybe he's lost his reason.' Shepherd just wouldn't let it go.

'He breaks out of a jail that's supposed to be escape-proof, gets through jungle that's supposed to be impassable and reaches the coast without friends, money or other help. Then, presumably, he manages to hole up somewhere till he can get a boat back to England. Probably works his passage on some flag-of-convenience freighter where they don't ask questions or demand papers. Anyway, the next thing we know he's on the bloody doorstep with a chilling little note about completing his contract.'

Smith paused, looked at Shepherd. 'Does that sound like a man who's lost his reason?'

'The last bit does. I still don't see why he had to tell us about it.'

'Because you can't see the reasons doesn't mean they don't exist.'

'Okay, you're his friend; to you he's a cross between Captain Marvel and Superspy. To me he's just another psychopathic killer. A nutter.'

'Have you ever worked with him?'

'Once. Years ago. I don't remember much about him.'

'He'll remember everything about you.'

'I'm flattered.'

'If it's to his advantage.'

'I think we've had enough about Abbott's character,' said the Controller, 'I'm more interested in his problems.'

Smith didn't agree – he thought the key to the situation lay in Abbott's character – but he let it pass.

'I mean, of course, his immediate problems,' the Controller went on. 'Money, food, shelter.'

'If he has enough of the first he can buy the rest,' said Smith.

'Then we'd better check with his bank, first thing,' said Shepherd.

'We've already told them to let us know if he gets in touch. It's standard practice to keep tabs on an agent's bank account if he disappears.'

'But you thought he was dead.'

'True. But we were waiting for some kind of confirmation. There'd been no positive identification of the body, remember; and it was just possible he was lying up somewhere, hiding from Njala's police. Though as time passed even this possibility began to fade – till he threw his little bombshell of course.'

'So where could he go for money?'

'His parents are dead,' said Smith, 'and he has two sisters, both married and both living abroad, one in Israel, one in Canada. Other than that there's an ancient aunt in Cornwall and a couple of cousins up north – the addresses are on the list I gave you – but he hasn't seen them for years. As for his friends, they're mostly in the Service, like me.'

Shepherd rubbed a hand over his face and smothered a yawn. 'So that leaves the wife.'

'Ex-wife,' said Smith.

'Would she help him?'

Smith thought she probably would. But his instinct was to protect her from the heavy-handed Shepherd and deal with her himself. He chose his words carefully.

'I think she's too neurotic and unreliable to be able to help anyone,' he said. 'I doubt if he'd take the risk.'

'He's setting out to kill Njala and he's worried about risks?'

'About unnecessary risks.'

'Maybe this one *is* necessary. Maybe he's got no money. Maybe he's desperate. Maybe he's nowhere else to go.'

'Maybe, maybe,' said Smith. 'Maybe if my aunt had balls she'd be my uncle.'

'Frank,' murmured the Controller deprecatingly. He believed they were all gentlemen in the Department and should speak like gentlemen. He was an old man, brought up in a different age.

'Anyway,' Smith went on, 'you've already got the flat under surveillance.'

Shepherd felt in some obscure way that he had drawn blood. He smiled a slightly lop-sided smile, due to an old jaw injury.

'Maybe,' he said, 'there are too many maybes in the situation. But Mrs Abbott's the one certain link with him. So maybe I ought to have a word with the little lady. Maybe I'd learn something. You never know.' He smiled again. 'Yeah, maybe I would.'

'Don't harass her,' said Smith slowly and distinctly.

Shepherd's small eyes narrowed to slits.

'If harassing her will catch me a killer, I'll harass her.'

'Frank,' said the Controller, 'it's not for us to tell the superintendent how to go about his job.'

'I know how he goes about it, I've seen him go about it,' said Smith in the same even tone. 'And I will not have her terrorised.'

'The little lady a friend of yours – as well as the husband?'

'Yes,' said Smith, 'if it's any bloody business of yours.'

'Now gentlemen,' said the Controller, 'let us cool it, as they say. And concentrate on the problem of persuading Colonel Njala out of that damned hotel first thing in the morning.'

He turned to Smith. 'I don't think you've actually met him, have you?'

'No. Seen him at one or two embassy receptions, that's all.'

'Well,' said the Controller with a hint of something like malice, 'you've got a lot coming to you.'

He tried to remember the smell of meadowsweet in damp woods, the face of a girl he'd once loved and her mouth and other particular and pleasant things. He was trying to focus his mind on something outside the present.

Then they hit him across the kidneys with a rubber truncheon. They weren't especially skilled. They had not yet learned, for instance, how to hit the sciatic nerve so that the pain exploded in your head. Still, hitting you across the kidneys was bad enough. The last time they did it he pissed blood for three days.

The interrogation seemed endless. He was a British agent, wasn't he? They knew he was, so he might as well admit it. What was his mission? Who gave him his instructions? How did he contact them? What code was he using?

And all the time he was trying to focus his mind on another time, another place. The trick, if you succeeded, was to stand outside yourself as it were. Then it wasn't really you screaming.

The rubber truncheon hit him in the face.

A Polish girl once told him he had nice white teeth. He spat one of them out with some blood.

He felt he was losing consciousness.

'I remember,' he said thickly, 'I really do . . .'

'What? What do you remember?'

They leaned closer to catch the muttered words.

'The smell of meadowsweet in damp woods,' he said, and they hit him again.

7

THE man all the fuss was about was sleeping with a girl in his penthouse suite high above Park Lane, though sleeping would be a wildly inaccurate euphemism.

Everything about Modibo Njala was larger than life – his personality, his prowess with women, his intellect and his barbarism. The effect was that of a comic caricature, except to those who knew enough to know there was nothing funny about him and a great deal that was deadly. He was a big man with appetites in proportion and the energy and means to feed them. He was always hungry for something or other. His sexual tastes were catholic – oral, anal, even normal, as the mood took him.

After making love to the girl in a variety of ways and positions he retired to the penthouse dining-room to eat an enormous bowl of Weetabix and cream and read through a résumé of the royalty negotiations he and his economic advisers were conducting.

Then he went back to bed, woke the protesting girl and started making love again, though this time a little absent-mindedly.

'Christ,' she said, 'don't you ever stop?'

'What's twenty-three per cent of two point seven millions?' he said, opening her legs. 'Six hundred thousand shall we say?'

'Ow,' she said, 'that hurts.'

'Perhaps you would like some Weetabix. It's very good for you.'

'I'd like some sleep. That would be even better for me.'

'You sleep your life away,' he said, looking down at her and settling into a rhythm. 'I don't know what's the matter with young people these days.'

Afterwards he let her sleep and slept himself for a couple of hours. Then he got up, had another bowl of Weetabix, read through the résumé again, worked out more figures and then spent an hour dictating memos and messages on a dictaphone.

By then it was getting light and he went out on to the roof garden, which overlooked Hyde Park. A pearly ground-mist was rising from the grass and the trees were gleaming wet and black after the night's rain. A solitary rider trotted in Rotten Row, an even more solitary man in evening dress looked incongruous walking through the soft sarcastic light of dawn, and directly below Njala the few cars going down Park Lane looked like Dinky Toys. London, not yet awake, seemed to lie under a peculiar and expectant hush.

Njala took a deep breath of morning air. He felt it was going to be a great day for him and made a mental note to check his horoscope.

He became aware of the cold – he was wearing only a bathrobe – and started to shiver. He went inside and had a bath as hot as he could bear it, then dressed leisurely.

Njala liked England. In some ways he felt it to be his spiritual home – he was educated at Eton and Oxford – though he still wore voodoo beads under his carefully laundered shirts.

When he went back to Africa he became a revolutionary overnight, not because he hated British colonial rule (he thought it benign compared to the French) or because he passionately believed in the freedom of his native land (he thought most of his black brothers were ignorant savages unfit to rule themselves), but simply because his broad nostrils sniffed the wind of change. And sniffed it early. If there was going to be a black take-over in Africa then Modibo Njala was going to be right up front where the action was.

At seven-thirty breakfast arrived with the morning papers and the mail brought by Arthur, his personal secretary and uncle of a former mistress. Njala had had many mistresses and his civil service was swollen with incompetent uncles. Arthur, however, was different. Arthur was competent. He was also intelligent enough not to appear so. Njala distrusted too much competence and intelligence in those around him.

'There's a Mr Smith waiting to see Your Excellency,' Arthur said.

'Smith? What an unlikely name. Especially in a hotel like this. Perhaps it's his real name.'

Arthur looked blank.

'That, Arthur, was supposed to be a joke. You were educated here, I'd have thought you'd understand. Well, who the hell is he?'

'I gather he's connected with the Ministry of Defence, sir. Something to do with Security.'

'Counter-Intelligence. What can they want, I wonder? Oh well, we'll see him after breakfast.'

'Sir, he has been waiting over half an hour.'

'They kept me waiting fifteen years, Arthur. And mostly in jail.'

He put a spoonful of cereal in his mouth.

'I am at breakfast,' he said.

While he ate he went through his mail, dictating answers on the dictaphone where answers were required, giving instructions about invitations to various functions and about his agenda for the day, which was always arranged to allow him two hours' sleep from six to eight in the evening (a further two or three hours was as much as he usually got or needed).

Arthur also gave him the latest oil-production figures, which pleased him.

'Seventy thousand barrels from the new field. Call it ten thousand metric tons. Excellent. The more we can sell them before they dig their own out of the North Sea the better. Mind you, they've mortgaged production for years to come.'

Njala was anxious to cash in on the oil bonanza while it lasted and was astutely undercutting the Arabs. This, with the uranium concessions, made him a valuable ally. It also made him a rich one.

He poured himself more coffee and said, 'Right, better have that chap sent up – oh, and order some breakfast for

52

Ermyntrude in there, then get her out of it. Give her some money and tell her I'll see her tonight.'

'I believe we are seeing another Ermyntrude tonight,' said Arthur.

'We are?' Njala frowned, trying to remember.

'The night porter's recommendation.'

'Oh, that Ermyntrude. The big smiling one. Yes, yes, of course. Best of the lot. I really like her.'

'Then I'll tell this one we'll ring her?'

'And not to ring us. Anything else I've forgotten?'

'The death warrants, sir. They're due to go out in the diplomatic bag today.'

'Of course, of course, our two young revolutionaries.'

'You've read the petition from their parents and relatives?'

'No, Arthur. Since I have no intention of pardoning them there is no point in reading the appeal. Unlike Christians I don't believe in the forgiveness of sins. Pardon them today, they murder you tomorrow. Why not? There have been several attempts already. I suppose my chances of being assassinated must be quite high.'

'Oh no, Excellency, I'm sure not. Apart from a lunatic fringe of extremists—'

'Everybody loves me. Yes, I know.' His tone was dry and disbelieving. 'Well, dictators do die in bed. But not many.'

He started to laugh.

'I don't know why I think that's funny, but I do. Where are the warrants?'

'In the pink folder, sir.'

'How inappropriate. Not even black edging.'

He took the death warrants out of the folder and studied them.

'And how old are they in fact, our failed revolutionaries?'

'One is eighteen, the other twenty.'

'Then they're lucky,' said Njala. 'They will die, as the Spanish say, with all their illusions.'

While he signed the death warrants with a pen that scratched loud and spiteful on the parchment, Arthur ordered breakfast for the sleeping Ermyntrude – Njala called all his girls Ermyntrude in a not always successful attempt at simplification – and asked for Smith to be sent up.

He waved the warrants about to dry the ink. He did not use blotting-paper because he felt that the ink, which was called permanent black, should stay as permanently black as possible. He felt it was appropriate. Having been educated in England he had a great feeling for the proprieties.

Smith was shown in by one of the Special Branch men on duty outside the penthouse.

Njala rose, gave him a brilliant smile and extended a hand.

'Ah, Mr . . . er. . . .'

'Smith,' Arthur prompted.

'Mr Smith. Of course. I apologise for keeping you waiting.'

'Not at all, Your Excellency.'

'But like the English I can't work without a proper break-fast. Coffee, Mr Smith?'

Arrogant bastard, Smith thought.

'No thank you,' he said with a polite smile.

Njala poured himself more coffee.

'Now Mr Smith, what can we do for you?'

Smith hesitated, gave another polite smile.

'Well, sir,' he said diffidently, 'it's rather awkward but . . . we have reason to believe someone's trying to kill you.'

'Kill me?' The pause was barely perceptible. 'Yes, that would be awkward. Do sit down, Mr Smith.'

The bastard was cool all right but that was to be expected. An attempt on his life was no new thing.

'Now, who is trying to kill me?'

This was going to be the difficult bit. This was where Smith had to walk lightly and tell part of the truth as if it were the whole truth. That was the important thing. Njala would expect lies, even accept lies, as long as they sounded like the truth. Plausibility was all. The name of the game.

Smith showed him a photo of Abbott.

'He escaped from one of your jails two or three months ago.'

'Ah yes, the Englishman.'

'Regrettably.'

54

'Who is he? I've forgotten what name was on his passport, but I assume it was false.'

'He's an adventurer, known under various aliases. The type who'll sell information to anyone if the price is right. He's done just about everything – smuggling, gun-running—'

'And spying.'

Smith nodded. 'He sold us some useless information once.'

'How interesting. You know him personally?'

'No.'

Smith knew he'd made a mistake. It is always better to stick as closely to the truth as possible, as every liar knows. However, it was a tricky question and a small mistake was better than a perceptible hesitation.

'You know what we thought? We thought he'd been sent to kill me.'

'By the Russians?' said Smith with a blandness that made Njala smile. 'That's possible.'

'And you think he's still trying to kill me?'

'According to certain reports we've received.'

'And the source of these reports?'

'That, I'm afraid, is classified information.'

'I thought it might be.'

'We also know he's in London. In fact the police and Special Branch are looking for him now.'

Njala stood up to indicate that the interview was over.

'Well, thank you for warning me, Mr Smith, though I'm sure you and the gentlemen from Special Branch will give me all the protection I need.'

'We will, we will,' said Smith. 'But not here, I'm afraid.'

'I beg your pardon?'

'This hotel. It's not safe. Too many entrances, too many people wandering in and out. From a security point of view it's hopeless.'

'Mr Smith, if you think I'm going to allow myself to be caged up in the embassy, to live like a celibate priest—'

'No, sir, nothing like that. We've got a very nice place in the country—'

'The country?'

55

He turned to Arthur, who had just entered after waking a drowsy and protesting Ermyntrude and arranging breakfast for her.

'He wants to send us to the country, Arthur, because he thinks some madman is trying to kill us. This one. Remember him?'

He pointed to the photograph of Abbott.

Arthur nodded. 'The English spy.'

Njala turned back to Smith.

'I loathe the country – those great draughty houses full of improbable people – every second person seems to be the son of a minor canon. And those horse-faced women. . . .'

'But it's only an hour's drive, sir,' said Smith, who was beginning to feel desperate. 'And you can invite any of your friends down. Any of them.'

'He means girls, Arthur.'

'In fact, apart from the nightclubs—'

'No, Mr Smith. The only other place I liked was Oxford, and I was a lot younger then. Eton was hell – full of bookmakers' sons. I love London, I'm happy in London, I'm staying in London.'

'But, Your Excellency—'

'And no madman is going to drive me out.'

'We can't assume he's mad.' Smith didn't know what to say.

'No? After two years in one of my jails he'll be a long way from normal, I can tell you that.'

Smith started to say something, then stopped. He had just caught sight of Ermyntrude standing in the doorway of the bedroom, sleepy and stark naked.

What the hell was he supposed to do? What was the protocol for meeting the naked mistress of a visiting head of state? He felt it must be laid down somewhere. Should he ignore her – pretend she wasn't there? Or say something – in French, of course, the language of diplomacy ('Enchanté, madame, de faire votre connaissance')? Anyway, he felt he should stand up in the presence of a lady, naked or not. He stood up. And gave a stiff little bow. That couldn't be wrong.

Njala and Arthur, who had been watching Smith in some surprise, turned and saw Ermyntrude at about the same time.

'Ermyntrude, my flower,' said Njala, 'what are you doing here?'

'Sorry,' she mumbled. 'Didn't know you had company.' She tried to stifle a yawn, but it escaped.

'Get her out of here, Arthur. And this time keep her out.'

Arthur took her by the hand and made encouraging noises, and she followed after him like a child sleep-walking.

Smith, who was a tall man, felt even taller and somehow ridiculous standing there while Njala, who was still seated, looked up at him. He sat down abruptly.

'Anyway,' said Njala, continuing as if nothing had happened, 'the hotel is stiff with policemen, and I really cannot see how I'd be safer in some crumbling mansion in the middle of nowhere.'

'For a start we'd be able to isolate it completely.'

'Just what I was afraid of.'

'From a security point of view, I mean. And it really is essential—'

'I'm sorry, Mr Smith – no, no, no. If you want to protect me, protect me here. In dear dirty old London.'

Abbott also got up early that morning and checked that the flat was still being watched, though by different men in different cars (the day shift, he presumed). He reckoned the watch would be taken off after a day or two or sufficiently relaxed for him to make the first of his planned moves without too much difficulty.

He made a short list of London's leading hotels and looked up their phone numbers, then had breakfast with Joan, listening politely to the staggering inconsequence of her chatter about office politics and amours (she worked in the actuarial department of an insurance company) and the way prices kept creeping up, a ha'penny here, a penny there, so that you didn't notice at first but after a time, my God. . . .

Abbott slipped his mind out of gear so that it coasted along without having to pay critical attention to what was being said. It was a habit he had developed after years of marriage and it came back to him easily.

She was chattering from a nervous compulsion to fill silences, which she hated and feared. She saw silence as a black emptiness in which relationships died from lack of words. She knew of course that relationships usually died from too many words, but like most people she never let the facts disturb a comforting belief.

He noted that she had done her hair carefully, made up her face and put on a clinging négligée that revealed the soft rounded lines of her body. It was a measure of her desperation. She always used to look a mess at breakfast-time. He felt suddenly sorry for her.

'You look nice,' he said. 'You really do.'

A mistake. A little pity is a dangerous thing.

The flow of chatter stopped. She looked at him.

'Christ,' she said, 'if you knew how lonely I get in these bloody barracks.'

'Surely you . . . have friends.'

An incautious remark but he was trying to deflect her attention from herself, and failing of course.

'Friends?' She gave what was meant to be a hollow laugh. 'My women friends, my *erstwhile* women friends, are married and don't trust me any more. They see me as a threat to *their* lousy marriages, God knows why. Maybe it's a kind of mid-Victorian hangover – you know, divorcees aren't quite proper and must be kept out of the marital home as well as the Royal Enclosure at Ascot. Which leaves me with two mad spinsters, one of whom smells of Irish stew. We go to the theatre and exhibitions together and have tea and talk about Art. Then I come back here and have a quiet scream down the lift-shaft, or get stoned. So much for women. Do you want to hear about men? You'll note I didn't say men *friends* because you can't be friends with men, they think we're not quite real somehow – know what I mean? Sort of temporary. Oh, they get stuck with us, but they *regard* us as temporary, somewhere between a purge and a nuisance. Maybe they're right too, maybe we should be kept in hutches at the bottom of the garden and just brought out for breeding purposes.'

She stopped, lit a cigarette and fiddled with the dead match.

'Sorry about that,' she said, 'but you did ask.'

She had a good mind once and now it was in disarray. He would have liked to help her but the one thing she needed from him, or thought she needed, was the one thing he was unable to give – his love.

She snapped the dead match in two. 'I must get dressed and get to work. Anything you want?'

'Can you lend me some money?' It was a relief to get back to the practical.

'I only have about ten pounds on me.'

'That'll do for a start.'

'How much more do you want?'

'I'm not sure. But two hundred should cover it.'

'Two hundred pounds? What do you want that for?'

'Hotel expenses mostly.'

'Can't you stay here?'

He shook his head. 'They might decide to search the place again. It's unlikely, but possible.'

She looked disappointed.

'Joan, love, I never intended to stay more than a day or two – just long enough to pick up some clothes and get hold of some money.'

She gave him ten pounds from her purse.

'I'll go to the bank in the lunch-hour.' Then, as the thought occurred to her : 'Couldn't you go to your own bank?'

He explained why he couldn't. 'But I'll give you a letter to my solicitor to cover the loan. He holds my power of attorney.'

'Yes, all right.' But she'd lost interest now that she knew he wasn't staying.

'I'll be late for the office.' She went to the door, then turned.

'I'm a lot easier to get on with than I used to be,' she said.

Her desperation was showing again. But what was there to say? There was a lie to say, there's always a lie to say. And perhaps it was the simplest, even the kindest thing to say.

59

'When I've got this other business straightened out,' he said, 'we'll talk about things.'

He had answered the unasked question that was hanging in the air. Anyway, he needed her co-operation, and the lie pleased her. Her face brightened, she smiled and went off to dress.

Well, there was little likelihood of her finding out the truth, unless the future took a very different turn from what he visualised. The future. Some future.

8

BY NINE O'CLOCK in the morning both the Controller and the Minister, after a desperate call from Smith, were trying to persuade Njala to leave the hotel.

The Controller paraded most of the arguments used by Smith, underlining the insecurity of the hotel and the necessity of moving to a safe house.

'And it really is necessary, Your Excellency. After all, when one of Her Majesty's Ministers of State decides it's sufficiently important to come here with me and—'

Njala held up a hand. 'Gentlemen, I'm overwhelmed by your concern.' He gave a thin quick smile. 'Unless it's all part of a deep plot to get the oil cheaper.'

The Controller's answering smile was slightly strained. 'Very amusing, Your Excellency, very amusing.'

'However, now that Mr Smith has failed and you have failed, who will you get to try next? The Prime Minister? Perhaps even the Queen herself?'

'At this point,' said the Minister, 'I'm afraid I shall have to insist on your following our advice. I really shall.'

The degree of crispness in his voice was nicely judged.

'Insist all you dam' well please, Minister, but here I am – and here I stay.'

Njala's voice had exactly the same degree of crispness.

'With the greatest respect,' said the Controller, 'I don't really think Your Excellency appreciates the danger he's in.'

Njala shrugged. 'Can you wonder? You have a report that this man is trying to kill me. A report that he's in London. Have any of your men seen him, spoken to him?'

'Well, no, but—'

'In other words, are you sure you're not being . . . well, oversensitive to rumour, to hearsay?'

'Quite sure, Your Excellency.'

'You know how these things happen, especially in security circles. A Russian trawler docks at Hull and MI5 send a couple of men along to keep an eye on it. The Russians find out the ship's being watched – and send a couple of their men to watch the watchers. This confirms MI5's suspicions – and more men are brought in. Until a full-scale, self-perpetuating security operation is mounted by both sides. Why? What are they trying to prove? That they are necessary. And that the money they spend and do not have to publicly account for is necessary.'

'Your Excellency,' said the Controller, beginning to understand Smith's desperation, 'we really do have the firmest grounds for our believing—'

He stopped as Smith entered.

'Excuse me, Your Excellency,' said Smith. He then said something in a low voice to the Controller, who nodded, grunted solemnly and turned to Njala.

'The, er, chap we were talking about now knows you're in this hotel.'

He was going to say assassin instead of chap but felt it would sound un-British and melodramatic.

'How did he find out?' said the Minister, who wasn't properly awake. Smith's entrance had broken an erotic daydream about the black girl in Fulham.

'He just phoned the big hotels asking to be put through to His Excellency.'

'But how can you be sure it was him?'

'Because we're having all calls to His Excellency monitored. Switchboard asked him to hold on, then I came on the line and asked him who he wanted. "Colonel Njala," he said, and spelt it out. When I asked him who he was he hung up. But I'm pretty sure I recognised the voice. Anyway, when I checked with the other hotels, it was the same story.'

'Why on earth didn't you tell the switchboard to say there was no one of that name staying here?'

'And block every official call, Minister?'

'Not to mention the unofficial ones,' said Njala.

'Sorry,' said the Minister. 'Not thinking.' He went back to his daydream.

'Now perhaps Your Excellency will understand the difficulties – and the danger,' said the Controller. 'If he can find you as easily as this. . . .'

He shrugged.

Njala was suddenly tired of the argument. 'Yes, yes, I understand.'

'Then you'll go to our place in the country?'

Njala, who was staring at Smith, said, 'Mr Smith is a clever man.'

It was an odd remark in an odd tone.

'I beg your pardon?' said the Controller.

'Very clever to recognise the voice of a man he doesn't know.'

'There's a very simple explanation,' Smith said quickly, having no explanation at all but hoping one would occur to him.

'Then save it, Mr Smith,' said Njala, losing interest, 'for one of those rainy days that come so often in these islands.'

For a moment Smith almost liked him.

The Minister, his forehead leaning on his hand so that it covered his eyes, was apparently deep in thought, but everyone knew he was asleep. He'd had a very tiring night for a middle-aged man.

When Alice got to the office she went immediately to Personnel. She had a week's leave to come and asked to take it from the following day. The suddenness of the request caused mild surprise in the Head of Personnel, but Alice made an excuse about wanting to spend a few days with her mother, who hadn't been well.

The real reason was that she wanted no part in the hunting down of Richard Abbott. Even if she didn't care for him any more, they had been close once, lovers once, however briefly. She wanted no remembrance of things past, no more mixing memory and desire.

She went into Smith's office and automatically turned the

desk calendar, noting that it was the last day of the cruellest month.

She typed out her notes of the emergency meeting and put them in a folder in the in-tray. She was about to leave when one of the phones rang. There were three on the desk, two going through the switchboard, one on an outside line, which was connected to a tape-recorder. This was the standard arrangement for all heads of section.

'Hallo?' she said. She heard the pips of a coin-box phone, then :

'Is Frank Smith there?'

She knew the voice at once. It was unmistakable.

'He's out, I'm afraid, but he's expected back soon. Can I take a message?'

She hoped her voice wasn't as shaky as her heart.

There was a silence at the other end; then, very quietly :

'It's Alice, isn't it?'

'Richard,' she said.

'How are you, Alice?'

'Fine. . . . How are you?'

It seemed crazy politely passing the time of day with a past lover, present assassin. But she didn't know what else to say, and she had been brought up to be polite.

'Tell Frank Smith I'll be in touch. All right?'

'Richard, wait a minute. Don't hang up. Please. . . .'

'Alice, if you're trying to have the call traced, you're wasting your time. It takes a lot longer than you think. And a lot longer than I intend to go on speaking.'

'Richard, I swear I'm not trying to have it traced. I couldn't if I wanted to. I'm alone in the office.'

'All right, I'll give you twenty seconds.'

'Richard, I wouldn't trick you. Really, I wouldn't.'

'What did you want to say?'

'I . . . well, I . . . want to talk to you.'

'What about?'

'Well, give me a moment. I mean, it's no good rushing me, I can't *think*. . . .'

There was silence on the line, then :

'Well?'

'I don't know. I just want to talk. Don't you understand?'

'Alice,' his voice was almost gentle, 'I can't afford to take chances.'

The line went dead. She sat there staring at the phone and trying to calm her heart by taking deep breaths and counting four before exhaling. It was something to do with Yoga or Rhythmic Breathing or something. She'd read about it somewhere. It was supposed to calm you down. But it didn't seem to do much good.

Then she remembered the tape-recorder. All conversations on the outside line were automatically recorded unless the machine was switched off manually.

She played the tape back. That didn't do much good either.

Then Frank Smith came in with the Controller and the Minister, now wide awake and jaunty at the success of their meeting with Njala, to which he had contributed nothing but his presence.

Alice told them about the call from Abbott.

'What did he want?' said Smith.

'To speak to you.'

'What about?'

'He didn't say. Just said he'd be in touch.'

'That seems odd,' said the Controller. 'Were you expecting anything like that?'

'No,' said Smith, 'except that you can always expect the unexpected from him.'

'How did he sound?' said the Minister. 'Strange? Unbalanced?'

'He sounded perfectly normal to me. But you can judge for yourself – it's on tape.'

She played the tape back for them.

'You sounded very emotional,' said the Minister.

'I was very flustered. I was trying to keep him talking in the hope that someone would come in – and I could signal them to have the call traced.'

She turned to the Controller. 'I'm sorry – but I just couldn't think of anything to say.'

'You also sounded very friendly,' the Minister persisted.

'I was trying to keep the conversation going, not cut it short.'

'And you called him Richard.'

She looked at Smith.

'I call him Frank,' she said.

'Oh,' said the Minister.

'That fact is, Minister,' said the Controller in his best old-school-tie voice, 'we're a pretty informal outfit – and she *was* his secretary for six months or more.'

'And,' said Alice, 'I liked him. He was nice.'

Smith suppressed a smile.

'Most of us liked him,' he said.

'Oh,' said the Minister again, not quite so jaunty.

'Mind you,' said the Controller, 'I don't believe he's the same man. I'm not saying he's certifiably mad, but I'm sure he's unbalanced.'

'That's possible,' said Smith.

Alice excused herself and went back to her office, glad to get away from them, glad especially that she was going on leave tomorrow and would no longer be involved in anything to do with Richard Abbott. Or so she innocently thought.

After she had gone the others listened to the tape again, speculated further about Abbott and his motives but came to no useful conclusion.

The Minister, who was thinking of that flat off the Fulham Road, discovered he had an appointment and left after once again congratulating everyone, especially himself.

Frank Smith was less enthused by the success, which had been only partial. Njala had made two conditions: that he would not leave till the following day and would not go more than forty miles from London – so that he would be within reach of visitors, especially the female ones.

So there was still the problem of guarding Njala that night (though he had promised not to leave the hotel) and of finding a suitable safe house and making it sufficiently secure sufficiently quickly. The details would be discussed with Shepherd later.

66

After Abbott had finished phoning from the coin-box in the entrance hall (in case Joan's phone was tapped) he went back to the flat and checked that the watchers were still there. He noted that they paid great attention to people going into the flats but virtually none to those going out, which was to be expected. Two of them were leaning against the car chatting to a third who was in the driving-seat. They looked relaxed and, judging by the occasional yawn, bored. The two men at the back of the flats also looked relaxed and were chatting and smoking. One of them blew a series of well-judged smoke rings. They obviously weren't expecting him to show up by daylight.

It occurred to him that if he walked out now casually talking to, say, the milkman or a woman neighbour, he would probably pass unnoticed. Anyway, they were unlikely to keep watch after tomorrow. One more night, to make sure, and they'd pull out. And if they didn't – well, he'd just have to find a way past them again. The main reason for staying where he was was to get the money from Joan. He'd still like to talk to Frank Smith though, and preferably not on the phone, but that might prove too difficult a problem. However, he was a man who sought simple solutions to difficult problems.

Frank Smith, the Controller and Shepherd, in conference in the Controller's office, also had a problem – several problems, in fact.

Smith and the Controller had picked what they considered a suitable safe house near Petersfield. It was a recent acquisition by the Department and so Abbott wouldn't know about it. It was a few miles outside the forty-mile limit set by Njala but they thought he'd be unlikely to quibble.

It was a big gloomy mid-Victorian mansion, Leyfield Hall, set in forty acres of partly landscaped, partly wooded grounds within a mile-long perimeter wall about seven feet high. Along the top of the wall ran a wire which, if cut or otherwise interfered with, set off an alarm in the house and in the lodge by the main gates.

Parts of the grounds were heavily wooded, especially near

the perimeter, and a number of trees, both inside and outside, overhung the wall. A team of workmen were already lopping and pollarding them. A slow-moving stream about ten feet wide and two or three feet deep curved through the grounds, entering by a low archway in the north wall, leaving by a similar archway in the west wall.

These were two weak points, which worried Shepherd. He had not yet seen the house but was studying a sketch-plan. Smith pointed out that a belt of woods outside the north wall also belonged to the house. Since the area was fenced off he suggested that guard-dogs should be let loose in the woods. Workmen were putting up a temporary hut close to the archway, which would be floodlit at night. A couple of armed men could be stationed in the hut.

'What about the other archway?' said Shepherd.

'As you can see, it's close to the main gates and the lodge and can easily be kept under observation. It will also be lit up at night. And I've asked one of our electronics experts to look at both archways to see if they can fix some sort of alarm system that will be set off by anyone trying to pass through.'

Shepherd nodded and grunted. 'Good. And inside the grounds?'

'We thought we'd leave that to you,' said the Controller.

Shepherd nodded again. 'Armed patrols with dogs.'

'But not running loose,' said the Controller. 'Njala and his guests might want to use the grounds if we get some decent weather, which is unlikely of course. Anyway, we don't want to give him the impression he's being caged up. So perhaps you can tell your patrols to be . . . well, a bit discreet.'

'He won't even see them. But they'll be around all right. And I'll have armed men in the lodge of course.' The Controller looked at him. 'Don't worry, they'll be discreet too. What about the servants?'

'Our own people. But they've been trained as servants – not guards.'

'That's all right, we'll look after the rough stuff, if any. Where will Njala have his rooms?'

'Here.' Smith pointed to the west wing. 'The whole of the upper floor on this side. The bedroom's here, at the back, with dressing-room, bathroom and so on. And here, with windows overlooking the front and side, is a nice big drawing-room. He'll probably also have his meals there, though there's a dining-room downstairs if he wants to get formal.'

'What about the meetings he's here for?'

'They'll be held in what used to be the music-room, downstairs at the back.'

'And what about his economic advisers and the other people, the ones who are negotiating for us? Where will they stay – at the house?'

'I think not,' said the Controller. 'There'd hardly be room. Anyway, Njala'll want the place to himself, apart from his secretary and the servants. I'll put the rest up at a country-house hotel about a couple of miles away.'

'As long as there's not too much coming and going.'

'There won't be. They'll be driven from the hotel to Leyfield Hall in the morning and back to their hotel in the afternoon, about four o'clock. Apart from that there'll only be the lady-friends.' The Controller smiled. 'Perhaps we can persuade him to stick to the same one for two or three days. That would cut the traffic down.'

'What's this?' Shepherd pointed to a small rectangle on the sketch-map.

'Summer-house,' said Smith.

'Overlooks the side where Njala's rooms are. I'll put Sergeant Clifford in there.'

'Bit trigger-happy, isn't he,' said Smith.

'Well, we don't want him *slow*, do we? And he's the best marksman we've got. Knock a flea off an elephant's ear.'

'Where do you want to stay yourself?' said the Controller. 'At the house or the lodge? Accommodation's no problem.'

'The house, I think,' said Shepherd. 'I want to be near Njala if anything goes wrong.'

The phone rang, and the Controller answered it.

'Speaking,' he said and listened. Then he said, 'Thank you,' and put the phone down.

'We've just had a report from the Southampton police that a man answering Abbott's description jumped ship from a Panamanian freighter the night before last. The freighter had come from West Africa.'

'That'll be him all right,' said Smith.

'Later the same night a wine store in the town was broken into and the till robbed of about fourteen pounds.'

'So where the hell is he now?' said Shepherd. 'Anyway, I'm asking the Petersfield police to report *any* crimes or misdemeanours, however trivial, to me while Njala's there. I don't want *anything* happening in that area I don't know about.'

'Good idea,' said the Controller.

'Another thing,' said Shepherd. 'I've taken the surveillance off his wife's flat.'

'Bit soon, isn't it?' said Smith.

Shepherd grinned. 'If he's half as cute as you say he is the chances are he'd spot my men anyway. So I've taken 'em away. To encourage him. To tempt him.' The grin widened. 'Then maybe I'll give him a little surprise.'

Abbott saw the men go just before noon and wondered about it. It seemed illogical to move them in the middle of the day, but he was aware that an illogical move, as in chess, isn't always what it seems. However, it solved one problem for him: now he could go out. And that might solve other problems.

Unbusy barmen tend to be chatty to generous customers around noon when there's little else to do but read the racing editions. So it wasn't difficult, after a quick pub-crawl in the network of back streets behind Park Lane, to find the pub where the night porter of Njala's hotel drank.

Night porters and love, as everyone knows, go together like a horse and carriage.

In any metropolitan hotel in the world if you want a woman ask the night porter (except in Moscow where, Intourist will tell you, whores don't exist. In which case stand outside the Moscow Hotel and flag down a prowling taxi.

70

The whore will be inside. If all you want is the taxi, ask her to get out. And politeness won't cost you a rouble).

Abbott, a much-travelled man, knew the importance of night porters and whores. And the night porter of Njala's hotel, even if the friendly neighbourhood barman hadn't pointed him out, wouldn't have been hard to spot – the heavy belly, heavy jowls, shiny face and shiny hair, and the braided trousers showing under his raincoat. Above all, that indefinable air of discretion and self-importance that sat on him like Eliot's silk hat on a Bradford millionaire.

The night porter, whose name was Osborn, ordered a vodka and tonic.

'Make it a large one,' said Abbott. 'On me, Mr Osborn '

The night porter turned and gave him a cold appraising look. His voice matched the look.

'I don't think I've had the pleasure.'

'George Wilson,' said Abbott, roughing up his accent. 'And to come straight to the point I'm looking for a job on the night staff of a hotel and I'm told—'

'Save your breath, Mr Wilson, and your money. We're fully staffed at the moment.'

He took out a pound note to pay for his drink.

'No, no, I insist. You see, you've got it wrong. I'm not looking for a job *now*. I already got one.'

He mentioned one of the big Paris hotels.

'Went there nearly a year ago – to learn the language. Year before that, Germany. Same idea.'

'Very wise, Mr Wilson, very wise. Especially in view of the Common Market.'

'And on top of that I've got a working knowledge of American.'

This brought a wintry smile to Osborn's face. Abbott raised his glass.

'Cheers.'

'Cheers.'

'Shall we sit down?'

They sat at a corner table and Abbott brought the conversation round to Njala.

'See from the papers he's with your lot. Last time he was in Paris *we* had him. What a headache.'

'Really?' Obsorn was giving nothing away. Abbott nodded.

'Girls all hours of the bloody night. Not much chance of a kip when His Nibs is on the town, eh? Which is six nights out of seven.'

Osborn smiled his naturally thin smile and said nothing.

A slim swarthy young man came in, ordered half a pint of bitter and smiled at Osborn.

'Hallo, Mr Osborn.'

Osborn acknowledged him with a barely perceptible, almost regal nod.

When he had been served, the young man smiled again.

'May I join you, Mr Osborn?'

His English was fluent and slightly accented.

'No, Kotiadis, you may not.'

The young man smiled once more to cover his embarrassment but anger showed in his eyes.

'Sorry, Mr Osborn. I didn't realise you were having a private conversation.'

'Some of these foreigners,' Osborn said to Abbott in a voice that was only slightly lowered, 'think they're everyone.'

'Couldn't agree more,' said Abbott. 'Jews and foreigners, you can keep 'em.' He smiled. 'And spades for that matter. And talking about spades, had any trouble with His Nibs?'

'I never have trouble with no one,' said Osborn in his dignified voice.

Abbott bought him another large vodka and tonic and tried to keep the conversation on Njala but learned nothing. Osborn was as discreet and as close as he looked, the little pimp.

Osborn finished his drink and said he must be getting back. He gave Abbott another thin smile and left, ignoring the young Kotiadis, whom Abbott joined.

'That was no private conversation,' he said. 'I'd never met him before. We just got chatting over a drink.'

'I bet you were buying them,' said Kotiadis. 'He's as mean as cat-shit.'

72

'Let me buy you one,' said Abbott.

Kotiadis said he'd have a bitter. Abbott told him the same story he had told Osborn about looking for a job in London. Kotiadis said to try the Savoy where he'd heard they were looking for night staff. He was a warm friendly youngster and talked freely about his home in Cyprus, his job under the hated Osborn, the hotel and its famous guests – including, of course, Njala and his string of girls.

Njala's favourite was a big dark smiling girl called Doris who hung around one of the bars off Brewer Street.

'What's so special about her?'

Kotiadis shrugged. 'Maybe because she'll turn out any time – two, three, four in the morning. Mind you, he's a spender. And Doris never could say no to bread.'

'Who can?'

The Minister left his office in the early afternoon and went to the Royal Marsden Hospital where his wife was dying of cancer in a room full of flowers. He was on his way to the flat in Fulham.

He sat by her bed trying to find things to say and trying not to look at her. She was emaciated, listless through sedation and leaden-hued. Her eyes were sunken and, he thought, shadowed by death. Her hair, once shining and black and her best feature, was grey and brittle.

Her name was Rose (Her face like a rose, Her mouth like a flower. Once. Oh yes, once, long ago). He remembered other things from the past and experienced a moment of biting sorrow. He cleared his throat and blew his nose and tried to be manly about it. He had loved her once, even though a good deal of that love was for her father's money (she was an only child). To be fair to him he did not realise at the time how much the money coloured his love. He had no more than the usual human capacity for self-deception.

She had a low sexual drive and he had amused himself with other women, though always taking care that she shouldn't find out (he wasn't just thinking of the money). Occasionally, from a look or a word, he wondered if she knew. But it was not a question he wanted to face, and he always slipped away from it or round it with a serpentine blandness wrought to perfection by years in the House of Commons.

Now he sat there in that flower-filled room uneasy with memories and awkward conversation.

He asked her how she was, and she said she still had trouble from indigestion. Whatever the trouble was had nothing to do with indigestion, but people instinctively hide behind some kind of euphemism in the face of death, either from dignity or fear.

'What sort of day have you had?'

'The usual. Pretty busy. Appointments. Meetings. You know.'

Which reminded him. He had another appointment. He looked at his watch. He would have to go. He got up, put his lips briefly to her damp forehead and went.

In the corridor he met the consultant whose patient she was. He made the usual inquiry and was told : 'Any time now. A few days. A week. Perhaps even tomorrow.'

He hurried out of the hospital and within a few minutes was pulling up outside the flat off the Fulham Road. He ran up the stairs and rang the doorbell impatiently.

'Who is it?'

'Me. Who the hell d'you think it is?'

'I had to know,' she said as she opened the door. 'I was about to get into a bath.'

She was naked apart from a pair of high-heeled slippers.

'Christ,' he said and went quickly in and shut the door.

'What sort of day have you had?'

'Don't say that,' he said.

She stood and looked at him in surprise. She was naked and healthy and beautiful, smooth-skinned and young. He could smell the youngness on her.

'Are you feeling all right?'

'Come on,' he said, taking her arm and pulling her towards the bedroom.

'In a hurry, aren't you?'

74

'So would you be if you were my age.'

'Your age? What do you mean? I've known men younger than you who—'

'Stop talking, will you? It's not the thing you're good at.'

*Solitary—the last refuge of a scoundrel. No, that was patriotism.
He giggled. His mind seemed to wander, take sudden turns and
jumps. He had hallucinations, dozed off into wild dreams. His
tongue was swollen with thirst. Perhaps he was going mad in the
twilight of that brick oven with its earthen floor, wooden bench and
small barred window high up in one wall.*

*Faces appeared in the gloom. The face of the first girl he had
kissed. Her Celtic pallor, her serious eyes. And the kiss, so romantic,
so emotional, so asexual in that dusk-filled room by the darkening
river. He was twelve years old and thought he would die of love
it hurt so much.*

*The moon-face of the Latin master, his gentle voice. . . . Don't
be too literal, Abbott, remember he's trying to tell us something
across two thousand years. The words are different but the feeling
is the same. . . . Odi et amo (in his clear schoolboy voice). I love
her and I hate her. Quare id faciam fortasse requiris? Why do I
do it perhaps you ask? Nescio. I know not. Sed fieri sentio. But I
feel it happening. Et excrucior. And I suffer. . . .*

*I suffer, I suffer, I am suffering. . . . Tears started down his face,
burning through the sweat, tears of anger. Not just against Njala,
but against the Department and the whole system that had used
him, discarded him and left him to rot in the back-end of nowhere—because the individual didn't count.*

*In the heat and the darkness his anger fed on itself and grew.
And sustained him.*

*But what sustained him even more, what nourished him like a
secret food, was the knowledge that ultimately his failure was of
no significance. The Department would never let go. Another agent
would be sent. And if necessary another. And another and another.*

Till one succeeded. Njala must die. It was written. Death's shadow was on him.

A comforting thought, a beautiful thought, a talisman that sustained him through the beatings, the humiliations, the weaknesses when he pleaded for mercy and wept like a beaten child. Even at his lowest ebb, when he was alone in the heat and darkness of that brick oven, dribbling blood through spit and swollen lips, it sustained him. Like music. Like the faint faraway music of victory hanging in the air over present defeat.

Then one day when he was taken for the usual interrogation and after the usual beating and the usual denials, his interrogators suddenly produced an English newspaper (with a flourish like a conjuror). The front page carried a two-column picture of Njala and the Queen. She was shaking hands with the bastard. Smiling at him.

There. Njala had become our friend. Our little friend. How about that?

And the interrogators smiled and said maybe they wouldn't have to beat him any more. And Abbott put back his head and laughed. And laughed. And his laughter was more terrible than his anger.

9

JOAN ABBOTT left the office at five o'clock and noticed the car parked outside at once. Anything parked in High Holborn in the rush-hour is likely to get noticed.

And nicked, she thought. And serve you right. She looked at the big heavy man leaning against the car. He straightened up and stepped in front of her and she found herself looking into a pair of flat slate-grey eyes. For a ridiculous moment she thought he'd picked up her unspoken thoughts.

'Mrs Abbott?'

'Yes?'

'Chief Superintendent Shepherd, Special Branch.' He showed her a warrant card, but she was too nervous to look at it properly.

'Could I have a word with you?'

'What about?'

'Your husband.'

'My ex-husband. We're divorced.'

Her nerve was recovering.

'Perhaps we could run you home – and talk in the car.'

'That would be nice.'

She knew Richard wasn't there. He had rung her just after lunch from a Mayfair pub to tell her the police watch had apparently been taken off the flat so he had gone out. He also gave her precise instructions about a phone call he would make in the evening to find out if the Special Branch men had come back.

The strength of Shepherd's casual grip on her arm made her nervous again – intimations of helplessness, of the prey in the grip of the predator.

Shepherd was thinking: Plump little pigeon, we'll break her down in no time.

He almost purred with pleasure as he opened the car door for her. She got in and saw a woman in a black two-piece costume in the opposite corner. Shepherd got in after her, squeezing her between himself and the woman.

'Woman Detective Sergeant Betts,' he said.

The woman turned and smiled, showing big teeth and small eyes which disappeared into slits. Joan Abbott began to feel nervous again. And she didn't like being pressed up against the woman, who was large-framed and bony and not disposed to make room. Between the two of them she felt very small and feminine and helpless.

The plain-clothes driver was not introduced to her. All she saw was the back of his head.

'Now,' said Shepherd, 'you know that Richard Abbott's in the country?'

'According to Frank Smith.'

'Has he tried to get in touch with you in any way?'

'He may have tried. He certainly hasn't succeeded.'

'You know he's wanted for questioning?'

'What about?'

'A security matter.'

The conversation drifted on, the questioning aimless rather than clever, and her volatile spirits began to perk up.

'May I ask you a personal question?'

'Certainly. As long as you don't expect an answer.'

Uppity, thought Shepherd. He said: 'Do you still love him?'

'Love, Superintendent – or should I say Chief Superintendent? – is a word to which everyone brings his own meaning. What happens to be yours?'

'I mean, would you take him in – shelter him?'

'Why, is he a criminal? Would I be harbouring a criminal?'

The car swerved suddenly and Sergeant Betts was thrown against her. She felt a hard elbow dig into the softness of her right breast.

'So sorry,' said Betts. 'Did I hurt you?'

Joan was sure it was an accident, but the apology and the

79

solicitous inquiry disturbed her for some reason. It was almost as if it wasn't an accident. She dismissed the thought as stupid.

They pulled up outside the flats and she said: 'Thank you for the lift, Superintendent,' and made to get out.

'A pleasure,' said Shepherd. 'Mind if we come in?'

'What for?'

'A few more questions.' He smiled. 'And a little look around.'

'You've already searched the place once.'

'Maybe we'd like to again.'

'Not without a search warrant.'

'Funny you should say that. . . .'

He produced a document and gave it to her and she felt herself going cold. She tried to look at it but the words were blurred. Nerves, of course. She must control her nerves. She handed the document back to him unread. She remembered the strength of the grip on her arm and the feeling of helplessness came back.

As she got out of the car she noticed that another car had pulled in behind it. Four plain-clothes men got out.

'Some more of my men,' said Shepherd. 'They'll do the searching. Don't worry; they're very tidy.'

And they were. They were very efficient too. Within a few minutes they were back with a bundle of filthy old clothes.

'We found them stuffed down behind the central-heating boiler in the kitchen.'

Shepherd sniffed. 'You can pong them from here.' He sniffed again. 'Do I detect meths – among other things?' He looked at Joan. 'Strange clothes for a nice lady like you to keep in the house.'

He waited for her to speak, but she couldn't. Her whole face tightened and became rigid, her throat constricted, her heart thumped in her chest. She couldn't take her eyes off the clothes.

'Waiting for the dustman, were we? To get rid of them?'

She still couldn't speak, still couldn't take her eyes off the clothes – old, ragged, filthy, evil-smelling, incongruous in the surroundings and somehow pathetic. They seemed to symbolise the underlying hopelessness of everything. To this favour must we all come.

'Lost our tongue, have we?'

The gentler his voice the more frightened she got. And the woman Betts was smiling at her. Those big teeth and tiny eyes and that mouth like a razor-slash.

'Well now, these clothes are tramps' clothes.' He turned to one of the men. 'Crossley, you were on duty here. Wasn't there some trouble with tramps?'

Crossley described how two of the tramps had started fighting while the others ran off. Shepherd listened in silence, nodding occasionally.

'And the one who ran round the back – did you see where he went?'

'Well, there's a passageway leading to the next street, he must've gone down there.'

'You saw him?'

'Well no, but—'

'Did anyone see him?'

'No, but he was running away. Running like hell.'

'And you know where he ran? He ran straight past that passageway, up the fire-escape – and into this flat. And it wasn't a tramp, it was Richard bloody Abbott.'

'No,' said Joan with a loudness that surprised her.

'No?'

'No.'

'Then I'm wrong,' said Shepherd, his voice if anything gentler. 'And you will tell us how these clothes got here.'

'Well, it was a sort of fancy-dress party,' she said uncertainly. 'And one of my guests. . . .'

She stopped, at a loss.

'Came dressed up as a tramp?'

'Yes, that's it.'

'And went home naked after stuffing his clothes behind the boiler.'

'No, well, you see. . . .'

Again she stopped. She felt panic rising in her like something alive and choking in her throat.

Shepherd stood up and looked down at her. Then he grabbed her, pulled her to her feet.

'Lying bitch!' His voice came out like a thunder-clap.

'Abbott's been here, hasn't he?' He gave her a savage shake. 'Hasn't he?' Another shake.

'*Hasn't* he?' She thought her head would come off. He half-thrust, half-threw her back into the chair.

'Answer me, you bitch, or I'll really start.'

She was too breathless to be able to speak. The Betts woman was smiling at her again.

'No,' she said when she got her breath back sufficiently. 'No, he hasn't.'

She'd hardly got the words out before he picked her up again, shook her again, threw her back in the chair again.

'You're coming down to the Yard.'

'On what charge?' Her voice shook, but she got it out.

'Harbouring a wanted man.'

'How was I to know he was wanted?'

'To say nothing of conspiracy, obstruction of the police and various charges under the Official Secrets Act.'

'I don't believe you.'

The woman Betts reached out and gripped her upper arm so hard it made her cry out. The grip was like a man's.

'Don't argue with the superintendent, dear.'

She had to stall, she had to wait for Richard's phone call so she could warn him. She had to find a way. . . .

'Look,' she said, 'I've been at the office all day. I must have a wash. And change my clothes.'

Shepherd was about to say something short and rude when he caught the Betts woman's impassive stare. He stared back with equal impassivity. Something passed between them, through the sort of deadpan communication system that develops between people who have worked or lived together a long time and who are fundamentally in harmony in certain ways.

Shepherd smiled. 'Of course, of course. No hurry.'

Joan, who had caught the look without understanding it, felt suddenly relieved, almost exultant. She thought she had won.

'I'll go and change.'

'One thing though,' said Shepherd. 'Sergeant Betts must go with you.' To Betts he said: 'Make sure she stays away from the windows. I don't want her giving signals or any of that malarky.'

Joan was going to argue but thought better of it. What did it matter? She was winning anyway.

She went into the bedroom followed by Betts and stripped down to pants and bra. She was going to strip completely but the way the Betts woman was staring at her made her feel unaccountably shy.

She went into the bathroom and started to wash. Betts leaned in the doorway, tall and angular, watching her with those tiny eyes that missed nothing.

'You've got a nice figure, dear. A bit plump – but in all the right places.'

She had intended taking her time over washing but found herself hurrying. She wanted to get out of that tiny bathroom and the overpowering presence of the other woman.

She dried herself quickly and dusted her shoulders with a scented talcum powder. Suddenly she realised the woman was close behind her, almost touching her. She half turned and saw the woman towering above her; she was almost as tall as Shepherd.

Don't panic, she told herself. Be calm. This is England, after all.

'Do you mind giving me a little more room?' The words were calm enough but the voice was breathy, with the suspicion of a shake.

The Betts woman bent her head and sniffed delicately at Joan's bare shoulders.

'Very sexy, dear,' she said, sniffing again. 'M'm, very sexy.'

'Will you *please* go away?' The shake in her voice was now distinct.

The woman didn't move. In fact she leaned closer. Joan

could feel her warm breath on her, then her hands on her. She screamed. It was the shock of being touched. The woman had merely put her hands on her shoulders.

'No good screaming, dear. No one's going to rescue you. Certainly not *him*.'

The grip on her shoulders tightened. The woman's strength felt enormous. She tried not to, but she could feel herself cringing. And that helpless feeling came over her, paralysing her will. She wondered if she was in a state of shock, removed from reality.

'He doesn't care what I do — as long as I make you talk. And if it helps to catch Richard Abbott, dear, he won't care if I rape you with a bottle.'

The woman spun her round like a top. The big face, big teeth, tiny eyes peering down at her and getting nearer, till she could see the downy hair on the long thin upper lip, even see a blackhead on the side of her nose, smell that warm cigarette-tainted breath, feel the grip of those big hands. . . .

Suddenly she felt a sharp pain in her left breast as if it had been twisted.

Chief Superintendent Shepherd heard her scream from the living-room. Then she burst in from the bedroom and ran straight into his arms. It was difficult to tell whether she was shrieking from laughter or fear.

Shepherd sat her in a chair and slapped her face. The old remedy. And it worked. Well, more or less.

The Betts woman came into the room and stood beside Shepherd and stared down at her. As soon as she saw the woman her lips trembled, and then she was trembling all over.

'Get her back into the bedroom,' said Shepherd, 'and get her dressed.'

'No,' said Joan, 'no. I won't have her near me. She's a sadist, a lesbian—'

'A lesbian? Sergeant Betts a lesbian? She's a married woman, a wife and mother.'

'A *wife?*' Joan started to laugh that shrieking laugh again. 'That's no lesbian, that's my wife. Oh my God.'

'She's hysterical,' said Sergeant Betts. 'Let's get her back into the bedroom.'

'No, please, *no*!' This time the shriek had no laughter in it.

Shepherd gripped her firmly by one arm, Betts by the other. They dragged her into the bedroom. ˙

'Get her dressed,' Shepherd said.

'It'll be a pleasure.'

The woman still held her tightly. Shepherd moved to the door.

'Please don't go,' said Joan. 'Please.'

She struggled impotently, ludicrously, like a fly in a spider's web.

'I can't stay here while a lady gets dressed.'

'I don't care about that, I'll dress in front of you, I don't care.'

'Mrs Abbott,' Shepherd sounded shocked, 'that would be most improper. Wouldn't it, Sergeant?'

'Most improper, Superintendent.'

'I'll lock the door, shall I, Sergeant? In case she tries to get out again.'

Joan tried to say something but was overtaken by a fit of sobbing and trembling.

'She's sweating. I'd better give her a bath. Shall I give her a bath?'

'Good idea,' said Shepherd, turning to the door. The Betts woman smiled at her.

'You'll find me very handy with the soap, dear.'

'I'll . . . I'll tell you . . . about Richard.' The words came out with difficulty between sobs.

She had broken. She had done her best but she had broken. In fact she had held out longer than might have been expected of someone of her temperament. She knew nothing of inter-rogation techniques or techniques for combating them. She was an amateur quickly broken by two professionals. She never had a chance. Later she would recover and try to undo some of the damage, but now she was broken.

Betts put a dressing-gown round her shoulders, sat her on

the bed and fetched her a stiff whisky. Her manner was brisk, impersonal, matronly. It was hard to believe it was the same woman.

The whisky made Joan feel better. The shivering was only spasmodic now.

Under Shepherd's questioning she admitted that Abbott had stayed in the flat the night before. She told him about the tramps – how Richard had bought them meths and got them drunk, changed clothes with one of them, then brought them along to the flats and engineered a quarrel between them.

'Clever,' said Shepherd. 'Very clever. He waits for us to search the place and put a watch on it, then finds a way of slipping past us.' He looked at Betts. 'On the assumption that we won't search it again. I like it. Oh, I like it.'

'He reckoned without you, though, didn't he?'

The Betts woman was smiling at him, almost simpering. Tiny eyes fluttering. Trying to look coy. Trying an impossibility, trying to cover those yellowing piano-keys that passed for teeth with her upper lip and *still* smile. Trying to *flirt*, for Christ's sake. Perhaps the lesbian bit was just an act. Sobering thought; but how far was she prepared to carry that act? Too far for me, Joan thought – but perhaps she was trying to rationalise her failure.

'Did he tell you what his plans were?'

'No.'

She was telling the truth and Shepherd realised it.

'When did he go out?'

'I don't know. He rang me from some pub after lunch to say the flat was no longer being watched.'

'Was he suspicious about that?'

'A little. He thought it was a day too early.'

'When's he coming back?'

'Some time this evening. He said he'd ring and let me know.'

'On this phone?'

'On the public phone downstairs.'

'Doesn't miss a trick, does he? And he'll be wanting to know if the coast is clear, won't he?'

Joan lowered her head.

'Won't he?'

'Yes,' she said.

'And you're going to tell him it *is* clear. Aren't you?'

He and Betts stood over her, stared down at her.

'Aren't you?'

She nodded listlessly without looking at them. Betts put a hand under her chin, lifted her head up, forcing her to look at them.

'Answer the superintendent, dear. Say yes.'

'Yes.'

Betts took her hand away and Joan's head fell forward again, like a puppet's.

They left her to dress and went into the living-room.

'Got him,' said Shepherd. 'Now we've got him.'

His face was shiny with excitement and triumph. Like Joan earlier, he felt he was winning.

They took him out of the darkness every day for exercise, and every day the light of the sun hit him in the face like a punch. He knew it was coming and kept his eyes tight shut but it went through his pale lids like a knife.

They marched him round a stockaded yard for ten minutes while the sun beat on him. Another form of torture. He was glad to get back to the gloom of solitary.

After (he guessed) about three weeks he found a nail in the yard and was able to scratch the passage of the days. He even scratched a chessboard in the earthen floor and played through games with imaginary pieces.

He had to occupy himself, had to hang on to his mind. . . . His mind. He sometimes saw it as a dark plain unfolding to infinity.

10

IT HAD BEEN a rough day for Frank Smith. After the broken night and the tiresome morning with Njala, he intended to slip home in the afternoon, put his feet up for a couple of hours and listen to some music.

But the afternoon brought trouble. Not serious but irritating to a tired man who wanted to go home.

Information had been leaked, presumably from the hotel's press office, about the sudden tightening of security around Njala and his intended departure to the country. The press wanted to know what it was all about. They got on to the Yard and the Ministry of Defence and got nothing but dusty answers. They scented a mystery and tried the Foreign Office, who first stalled them with a statement that was a masterpiece of obscurity even for the Foreign Office, then sent an urgent memo to Frank Smith, who could (and should) have dealt with it, but decided to put it on the Minister's plate. Let him earn some of that bloody money for once. Frank Smith was being petty and knew it. But he was feeling petty. It had been a rough day.

He rang that steeply superior private secretary, who said in his snootiest voice that his master was unavailable. That was the last straw.

'You mean,' said Frank Smith with a calculated and matey coarseness, 'he's still banging that black bird in Fulham? Doesn't he ever get off the nest?'

It must have taken the secretary's breath away because all he heard on the line was a kind of strangled splutter. He hung up and laughed, his temper restored.

Then he rang the Foreign Office and suggested a press conference later in the afternoon at which he would make a statement and answer questions.

The conference went off well. The statement, which was false but plausible, said the Government had wind of a rumour that an IRA terrorist group were planning to kidnap or assassinate politically important visitors to Britain during the spring and summer. Of course it was only a rumour, possibly even a hoax, but . . . Frank Smith spread his hands. There *had* been the Herrema kidnapping, remember.

And why was Njala leaving London?

To visit a friend in the country.

'Male or female?' someone asked. 'Or is that a silly question?' And there was a ripple of laughter from the men. The only woman journalist there sniffed.

Coming out into Whitehall afterwards the sunshine felt like a pleasant shock. It was the last day of April and overnight the weather had changed with suspicious suddenness from cold and rainy to sunny and warm. He tried to remember a line of Shakespeare's about the uncertain glory of an April day. There was a hint of thunder in the air though, and it made him uneasy.

His car was waiting and he told the driver to take him home. Along the Mall he wound down the window to look at the green grass and the girls in their summer dresses. They had come out with the sun, like flowers after rain. A yearly miracle that never palled. Looking at them, the lyric of hip and breast and thigh and swinging hair, he felt the old male desire for a woman. He lay back on the cushions and sighed and thought of Joan Abbott and her rounded softness. He supposed he shouldn't have taken no for an answer. Everyone knew that women said one thing and meant another. The trouble was (apart from those nagging guilt feelings about Richard) he had always been shy of women. He liked them, he wanted them, but he was shy of them. Of course sexual need harassed him out of the shyness from time to time, but the relationships were fleeting. Perhaps like most men he was afraid of emotional commitment. A sign of typical male immaturity. No wonder he was still a bachelor. He sighed again and continued to think of Joan Abbott.

He was still thinking of her as the car turned out of St

James's Street into Piccadilly, heading west. Just past the Ritz he yelled to the driver, 'Hold it!' and jumped out. He was sure he had seen Richard Abbott. But when he caught up with him he saw it was someone else. He got back into the car red-faced and breathless. Christ, I'm out of condition, he thought.

They drove slowly through the Piccadilly traffic and he watched the crowds on the pavement, the men rather than the women, automatically searching for Abbott, which was ridiculous but he couldn't help it.

When they got to Kensington Gore his mind was still alive with Abbott and just before Queen's Gate, where he lived, he told the driver to go on to the office. He suddenly wanted to listen to the tape of Abbott's voice again. Perhaps he'd missed some clue, some hint. Something.

But though he played the tape several times Abbott sounded as calm and rational as ever, and he learnt nothing. He called Alice in and asked her to listen, but she was no help. Not that she wanted to be. It was after five and she wanted to get home to the flat, wash her hair and do some minor but important domestic chores.

'I'm sorry, I'm keeping you.'

'That's quite all right,' she said politely, keeping her eyes down as usual.

She too had on a summer dress, and as she leant forward listening to the tape (in fact she was thinking about some tight jeans she was going to buy and not listening at all) he could see the beginning of the shadowed valley where the neckline ended and the suggestion of rising curves began. Twin roes feeding on Mount Gilead. It was warm in the office and he tried not to look.

She *was* attractive. It surprised him (for about half an hour a year he found her attractive and it always surprised him).

He started to listen to her voice on the tape – and something else surprised him : the emotion in it.

'You really did like him,' he said, switching off the tape.

'Yes,' she said, still looking down.

He wanted to ask her more, but did not know how to. His old shyness had come back.

'It's well past your time,' he said abruptly. 'I'll drop you home.'

In the car he still had the feeling that there might be more to know about her and Abbott. Perhaps it was due to his odd mood, the warmth of the evening, the closeness of her, the female smells he was suddenly aware of, the remembrance of the girls in their summer dresses along the Mall, his own vague sexual stirrings....

'Did he ever take you out?'

'Richard? A couple of times. When he was at a loose end.'

'Did he ever say anything that . . . well, might help us? I mean, was there anything . . . strange about him?'

He didn't really know what he meant.

'He always seemed normal enough to me.'

'What did you talk about?'

'I don't know. Ordinary things. I can't really remember.'

They drove on in silence along Holland Park Road. He looked out of the window. More girls in their summer dresses. Well, that wouldn't last.

'Did you ever. . . .'

He stopped. That damned shyness again.

'Have an affair with him?'

She turned and looked at him with those funny eyes.

'No,' she said and smiled. The lie came out easily, delivered with the aplomb of a politician. It surprised her. She had been brought up to be truthful as well as polite.

'And if I *had* had an affair with him?'

'I thought perhaps you might've learned something we didn't know.'

She laughed. 'I'm sure I would have. I *hope* I would have.'

'I'm sorry, I didn't mean that. I meant. . . .' He felt himself reddening. 'Forget it.'

The car stopped. She thanked him and jumped out.

'I wouldn't have minded,' she said. 'Having an affair with him, I mean.'

And ran up the steps to the front door.

Her legs were quite something, Smith thought, not for the first time.

It's time he had a woman, Alice thought as she let herself in and called to the canary in a trilling voice: 'Mummy's home, Solly. Mummy's home.'

The canary was called Solomon because she thought it looked wise and slightly Jewish. And though it sang rarely it sang with great feeling. The Song of Solomon.

The moment he stepped inside the flat and closed the front door behind him the feeling of unease that had been with him all day lessened. The tensions relaxed as they always did when he got home. The general spaciousness, the elegance of the expensive and carefully chosen furnishings, the comfort, the quietness, the light from the tall Regency windows, all combined to please and reassure him.

He sighed happily, put his briefcase on a Sheraton side-table and went into the sitting-room to get the shock of his life.

Sitting in a wing-chair facing the door was Richard Abbott.

'I said I'd be in touch.'

He could hardly believe it, but the face of course was unmistakable – square and bony, now even bonier, making the dark eyes darker and deeper set. And the *moderato* voice with its slight rasp.

He didn't know what to say or do. Particularly what to do. But he felt he ought to do something. He looked at the telephone, which he saw had been moved to an occasional table by Abbott's chair.

Abbott took in the glance and shook his head.

'Please, Frank,' he said, 'don't do anything hasty.' He let his jacket fall open, revealing the gun in its shoulder-holster. 'Prevention might not have a cure.'

'You'd shoot me?' Frank Smith found his voice at last. 'You'd actually shoot me?'

Abbot thought about it.

'No,' he said, 'if it came to it, I don't suppose I would.' Then his mouth curved into the beginnings of a smile. 'But I'd hate to be wrong.'

'And if I tried to walk out – or use the phone?'

'I'd have to restrain you. After all, I'm younger than you and fitter. I even remember some of the unarmed combat Sergeant Evans taught us. Do you?'

'All I remember is *you* telling me a kick in the balls was worth all the Kung Fu in China.'

Suddenly both men found themselves smiling at each other, reviving old memories, old affections. Then the reality of the situation came back and with it an edge of wariness.

'What do you want, Richard – money?'

'No.'

'You've got money?' Smith sounded surprised.

'Bob or two.'

'Well . . . what about a drink, then?'

'Later perhaps.'

'A coffee?'

'No thanks.'

'Bite to eat – a sandwich?'

'Knock it off, Frank.'

'What do you mean?'

'The old elimination process. If he's got no money he can't be at a hotel. That means he's either living rough or staying with a friend. And if he's had a shave and isn't hungry he can't be living very rough.'

'So you're staying with a friend.'

'I'd tell you of course.'

'You've already done the eliminating for me.'

'All you have to do is find the deliberate mistake.'

The two men stared at each other. Smith decided he was getting nowhere.

'Richard,' he said, 'what *do* you want?'

'A word.'

'Hell of a risk to take for a word.'

Abbott shrugged. 'I thought I'd like you to know, since you were a friend—'

'Still am, aren't I?'

'Or at least be able to see for yourself that I'm not as crazy as the Department and the bloody politicians no doubt think I am.'

'Does it matter what they think?'

'It matters what you think.'

Smith could see nothing about him that suggested insanity or lack of balance, but perhaps appearances were up to their old tricks. One thing he was sure of. Abbott hadn't come there merely to try and prove something.

'So you've come back for your revenge?'

'Revenge?' Abbott looked surprised. 'There's more to it than that. A lot more.' He paused. 'I was given a job to do. I want to finish it.'

'That sounds pretty crazy for a start.'

'Anyway, if it was revenge I wanted, it would be revenge on the Department.' He paused again, looked directly at Smith. 'For blowing me.'

Smith drew his breath in sharply. It was his turn to look surprised. He hoped he was convincing.

'Blowing you? What are you talking about? You were blown by your local contacts.'

Abbott's mouth curved but didn't quite make the smile.

'So that's the story they put round the Department.'

'Story?'

'Those local contacts could only have blown me on orders from London.'

'What do you mean?'

'They didn't even know of my existence – unless London told them.'

'Are you saying you never got in touch with them – as you were supposed to?'

Abbott's mouth curved again, still not making the smile.

'I don't follow orders automatically. I think about them. And on the flight over I decided to work alone. It might be more difficult but I thought it would be safer.'

'All right – but why should London blow you? And to Njala of all people?'

'Because at the last minute, just before I was due to put a

boat-tailed bullet into the bastard, London did a deal with him – for oil, uranium and God knows what. All of a sudden he was our little friend. So stop everything stop the assassination. Above all, stop Richard Abbott.'

'That's guesswork.'

'But London couldn't stop me because they couldn't get hold of me. So you sent a message to the local contacts—'

'I did no such thing.'

'Not you personally, Frank. The Controller. Or someone higher still.'

Frank Smith shook his head emphatically. 'I was your co-ordinator. All messages would have been sent through me.'

This time Abbott's mouth actually made the smile. It was small and sad.

'No, Frank, they wouldn't send that kind of message through a friend.'

'What kind of message?'

'The kind that has the famous fail-safe clause that stops everything. It certainly stopped me.'

'Richard, you're talking in riddles.'

'In other words, if the local contacts couldn't find me in time – and of course they couldn't – they were to make an anonymous phone call to Njala's police.' The small sad smile came again. 'I was blown all right – all the way from London.'

'You're guessing, Richard, just guessing.'

'But guessing good.'

Too good, Frank Smith thought. Much to good, matching his own guesses, which Smith nevertheless couldn't accept without destroying his one remaining article of faith : that the Establishment, for all its faults, was run by Decent Chaps and therefore fundamentally All Right. So, despite his intelligence and scepticism, he pushed his ugly guesses away, into some mental limbo. Anyway, there was no evidence.

'Anyway, there's no evidence.'

'Those local contacts would be pretty good evidence. If they weren't so conveniently dead.'

'Look, I admit certain happenings, certain coincidences are mysterious, even suspicious, if you like—'

'They're bloody suspicious. And I don't like.'

'But there's still no evidence, no facts.'

'Oh, there are facts all right, if you know the whole story. But you only know part of it. And you've probably forgotten most of that.'

'I remember the hell of a time we had persuading you to take on the job.'

'What did you expect? I wasn't some contract killer with a fast gun and no imagination. You could've picked that kind up for a few thousand quid in Caracas or Maracaibo – with his SS number still tattooed on his left arm.'

'The Department doesn't employ war criminals to—'

Smith stopped short of the coming incongruity.

'To commit murder for them – only decent chaps?'

Abbott laughed without amusement. 'O tempora, O mores. What do you remember of the operational plan?'

'Not much because the details were left to you. But I remember you were supposed to kill him on Independence Day.'

Abbott nodded. 'His big day. The day he takes the salute at a march-past in Njala Square – togged up like a Christmas tree. Then he goes on a river trip so that the crowds who couldn't get into the square can line the banks and cheer and strew flowers on the water. A day of royal progress and public love.'

Abbott smiled his small smile. 'A good day to kill him.' He got up, wandered to the window. 'Any day would be a good day to kill him.'

His eyes searched the street below, the roofs and buildings opposite.

'Think I've got the place staked out?' said Smith, smiling.

'Habit,' said Abbott. 'It's automatic. Almost a reflex.'

He turned away from the window, but remained standing, and off-handedly watchful like an animal.

'I had it nicely set up. I took a third-floor flat overlooking a bend in the river. And however the boat came out of the

98

bend I'd have a full frontal of him for about twenty seconds. All I'd have to do was line up the cross-hairs of the Leatherwood 'scope on his big black heart and squeeze the trigger. A pushover. At least it should've been.'

Frank Smith thought for a moment. 'Richard, looking back, are you sure there wasn't some kind of hint that something might be going wrong?'

Abbott shook his head. 'It was all plain sailing. I went there to work – and I worked. And nobody could prove any different.'

Abbott had arrived two months before Independence Day as a freelance geologist doing mining surveys for an international finance company. The cover was genuine – he had worked as a geologist in Africa before the Department recruited him. The finance company was less genuine. It existed, with a registered office in the Bahamas, as a front for SIS operations.

'And there couldn't have been anything wrong with our communications – because we didn't have any.'

After landing at Njala Airport, Abbott had sent one coded cable to the Department (via the Bahamas) announcing his arrival. And that was all. If anything were to go wrong subsequently there would be no traceable connection with London. Political assassination was a weapon of the KGB, the CIA and terrorist groups, not the British government. Such a thing was unthinkable and must stay unthinkable.

'What about the gun?' said Smith. 'Could that have been spotted in transit?'

'Only if they'd opened the diplomatic bag,' said Abbott with some weariness. 'And that would've caused an international incident. In spades.'

The gun, a knock-down sniper's rifle based on the Armalite 15, had been brought in in the diplomatic bag, packed into a suitcase by the embassy's military attaché and left in a luggage locker at the airport. The key to the locker was mailed to Abbott, poste restante, under an assumed name.

'So, as far as you knew, everything was fine?'

'Couldn't have been better. Went like a wedding – till the

morning before Independence Day.' Abbott's tone became dry. 'That's when it all hit the fan.'

He sat down abruptly and stared at Frank Smith.

'Just after dawn I heard a noise like a bomb. It was Njala's police kicking down the front door. They came in like a herd of buffalo, pulled me out of bed, kicked me around a little and asked where I'd hidden the gun.'

'I said: "What gun?" And they kicked me again. Then they tore the place apart looking for it. They had the floor-boards up, the backs out of cupboards and the stuffing out of everything, including me. In the end they started knocking down the partition walls. But they still couldn't find it.'

'Where on earth was it?'

Abbott smiled his small smile again. 'Up a gum tree, would you believe, in Njala Park. Wrapped in oilskin.'

'Clever.'

'So how did they get on to me, Frank?'

Smith spread his hands. 'We couldn't have told them, we didn't know where you were.'

'My cover-name would've been enough. Like all foreigners I had to register with the police. London knew that.'

Smith was silent, searching for a reason.

'I still think it's possible you made a slip — drew attention to yourself in some way.'

'How? I'd been there two months coming and going, making survey trips into the bush — but always with native porters and guides and a load of surveying gear. And the surveys were genuine, what's more. So were the reports I filed to that phoney office in the Bahamas — with copies to Njala's Ministry of Mines, as per regulations. I couldn't have acted more correctly or openly.'

'Look, you know how suspicious they are of foreigners. Maybe you had a drink with the wrong stranger in the wrong bar. Something trivial. Something you wouldn't even remember.'

'I remember everything. And I don't drink in back-street bars with strangers. I don't even get into conversation with them, and I'm bloody suspicious if they get into conversation with me. I know how to keep my nose clean, Frank, I've had a lot of practice.'

'What about all those crooked officials? The place is stiff with 'em. Maybe you bribed the wrong one, or didn't bribe one you should have.'

'West Africa's my territory. I know who to bribe, when to bribe, how much to bribe.'

Smith spread his hands again. 'I'm simply looking for an explanation.'

'Unlike Njala's police, you're looking in the wrong direction. They knew what they were looking for. Because they were told.'

'That's what you *assume*. But you don't *know*.'

Abbott's smile grew smaller and ever sadder. 'If you were in my place, Frank, and taking into account all the circumstances, what would you assume?'

'Exactly what you do, no doubt. But that doesn't make it right.'

'A nice answer, Frank. You should've been a politician.'

'Richard, you must admit there's a possibility, however remote it may seem, that you're wrong.'

'Oh, there's a possibility, but—'

Smith held up his hand. 'Hold it right there. And let's have that drink. It really is time.'

Abbott shrugged. Smith was stalling, searching for excuses that didn't matter. If only he knew how little they mattered. But of course they did matter – to him. Old Smithy, holding up the Establishment to the last, or holding up his belief in it rather.

Smith took a bottle and two glasses from a cupboard.

'Who was it said it's the duty of all wine to be red? This is a Marcillac from a place called Conques in south-west France. I once drove two hundred miles in a day to pick up a case. . . .'

He went on talking about the wine automatically. He wanted time to think, time to find a way to undermine Abbott's control of the psychological as well as the physical situation.

'The only French wine made from the *pinot noir* grape

outside Burgundy. Cheap too. Six francs fifty a bottle.' He raised his glass. 'Cheers.'

They sat sipping the wine in that elegant room with the evening sun slanting through the long Regency windows, aware of an occasional hum of traffic from Queen's Gate. A peaceful and civilised setting in which they should have gone on talking about wine, Smith felt, or women or poetry or the decline of the novel. Not murder.

'Richard, we know all governments get up to dirty tricks, but I simply cannot believe our government would deliberately, cold-bloodedly hand you over to be tortured or murdered just for some trade and political advantages.'

'Well, that's where our views of the Establishment differ. Anyway, there was nothing deliberate or cold-blooded about it On the contrary, they temporised and rationalised and generally fucked about, like all committees, till a decision was forced on them.'

'A committee? What committee?'

'I don't know. But it's bound to have been decided by a committee. Of Defence chiefs or Intelligence chiefs or whatever. They're never too bright but at least they're gentlemen. Except for one. There's always one who's *very* bright – and not quite a gentleman. And he's the one who said, "The only way out is to blow the poor bastard." And all the gentlemen threw up their hands in horror and said, "Decent chaps don't do that sort of thing." And the bright one said, "Wait for it, wait for it – we hand him over, then we buy him back. We make it a condition of the deal with Njala that we get our agent back. Like getting your ball back when it's gone over next door's wall." And after the port had passed round a couple more times everyone thought it was a splendid idea.'

Abbott finished his wine.

'You're right,' he said, 'it's nice. Can I have another?'

Smith poured him another.

'Look, Richard—'

'The trouble was. Njala wouldn't play. Why should he? He held all the aces. And though he admires fine old English gentlemen from a safe distance he doesn't trust them. And can you wonder? First they stick him in jail as a political agitator, then they set him free and smile on him. Then they try to murder him. Now they're smiling on him again. Even a hard man like Njala must feel a shade uneasy. So he holds on to every advantage – and every hostage.'

Frank Smith was standing with the wine bottle in his hand. He poured himself another glass and sat down.

'Richard, what you're saying is still largely supposition, and there's still the possibility, as you yourself admitted, that you're wrong.'

'About London having blown me, you mean?'

'Yes.'

Smith felt he'd made a good point at last. He sipped his wine. It was smooth and clean over the palate with an after-taste of fruit.

'What difference does that make?'

'All the difference in the world, surely?'

'Frank, the point's academic. I thought I'd made it clear I'm not acting simply out of revenge.'

The wine seemed suddenly to go sour in Frank Smith's mouth.

'Then what are you acting out of? Conviction?'

Abbott nodded slowly. 'The conviction that Njala deserves to die. A conviction that you and the Controller went to great pains to plant in me. After all, I'm only carrying out the Department's policy.'

'Richard, that was over two years ago. The policy has changed, times have changed, circumstances have changed, attitudes have changed, everything's changed. . . .'

'Except Njala. The one constant in the whole equation. And he's the same. The same killer, the same tyrant, the same fascist—'

'Not that word, Richard, it's on the lips of every teenage hooligan with a grudge against society and every Big Brother who rapes his little neighbour.'

'You were quick enough to use it. You and the Controller at that pleasant country house by the Thames. He's a fascist. Totally ruthless, totally irresponsible. He'll start a war in

Africa, like Hitler in Poland, like Mussolini in Abyssinia. Kill one man and you'll save thousands, maybe millions if the Russians and the Americans come in. . . . And so on. And so on.'

'We did have a case, you know. There *was* a risk of war. A terrible risk.'

'There's always a risk of war. It's like the pox.'

'I mean a specific risk. From a specific situation. But fortunately, at the last moment, he changed his mind.'

'And tomorrow he'll change it again. Or next week. Or next year. And there'll be another crisis, another situation. Well, won't there?'

Smith made no attempt to answer.

'Listen, if it was right to kill him two years ago, it's right to kill him now. Unless the whole thing was expediency.'

'Maybe,' said Smith slowly, 'it wasn't right to kill him two years ago.'

'No? Well, you convinced me it was. He deserves to die, you said. The Controller said. You all said. And you were right, and I tell you this.' His tone was easy, confidential. 'He's going to die.'

'You know the harm you'll be doing the country?'

'I know the harm the country's done me. And now the country will have to face the consequences of its actions – just like the rest of us.'

'Richard, all you're trying to do is justify a murder.'

'No, Frank. It's already been justified. By you and your masters. Only you don't call it murder, of course.'

Frank Smith drank some more wine in silence. It was impossible to argue against that sort of simplism.

'All right, you've got a case, all right, Njala deserves to die, all right, governments should be held responsible for their actions, all right, all right. . . . But why you, Richard? That's the bit I can't get over – appointing yourself God or Nemesis or Jupiter hurling thunderbolts from the sky. I mean, it's *not* you, is it? Not you at all.'

'You're clouding the issue. I'm not acting like God or whatever, I'm simply going to kill a man.'

'Oh, great.'

'The Russians and the Asians and people like Njala do it all the time. Because they haven't been conditioned by the Western Christian ethic about the sanctity of human life.'

'But you have.'

Abbott smiled. 'Maybe that's what worried the Controller. Maybe that's why he ordered those psychological tests — to find out if I needed a glass of water.'

'A glass of water?'

'The man Stalin sent to murder Trotsky lost his nerve at the last moment and had to sit down and ask for a glass of water. Did you know that?'

'He still buried the ice-pick in Trotsky's skull. Anyway, you don't really think the Controller doubted your nerve, do you?'

'I think he doubted everyone's nerve. He had several other agents tested at the same time, you know.' Abbott's dry voice went even drier. 'And I got the coconut.'

Frank Smith lit a cigarette, his first of the day. He had been trying to cut down and made a rule not to smoke before six o'clock. But rules were made to be broken, as the French said or someone said.

He felt he had to make one last appeal, knowing as he spoke, looking into the blackness of Abbott's eyes, that it was hopeless.

'Richard, you don't have to go through with it. I could fix things. . . .'

Abbott spoke slowly. 'I do have to go through with it, Frank. It's all I've got left, the only thing that gives point and purpose to my life. And everything else is secondary.'

Well, he had tried. He knew it would take more than words to stop him, more than a civilised chat over a glass of wine. It would take a gun to stop him. Ashes to ashes, dust to dust, violence to violence. The old solution, the only one that never goes out of fashion. The Germans had a saying, *Unkraut vergeht nicht* — weeds never perish. Nor does violence. The history of man is the history of killing.

Smith sighed and extinguished his cigarette with his hopes. He liked Abbott, had liked him for fifteen years.

'Some more wine?'

'No thanks.'

'Coffee? What about coffee?'

Abbott knew that Frank Smith, like many bachelors, took an almost old-maidish pride in minor domestic achievements.

'I still grind it fresh, you know. None of that instant rubbish.'

Abbott smiled. 'All right.'

Smith went happily into the kitchen and busied himself with the beloved ritual, occasionally humming off-key tunes that had been popular during the war. Once or twice he shouted a remark to Abbott but got no reply. When the coffee was ready he poured it into two very thin Royal Worcester cups. He smiled with pleasure. The aroma was delicious. He put the cups and a plate of petits fours on a tray which he carried carefully to the sitting-room.

As he opened the door he said, 'You know, the trouble with most people when they make coffee—'

He stopped. The room was empty.

11

HE PICKED UP a cab in Queen's Gate almost immediately. By the time Frank Smith had gone through that complex coffee ritual he'd be halfway down Piccadilly.

In the entrance hall of the flats Joan Abbott, flanked by Shepherd and Betts, waited for Richard to ring.

Shepherd had moved fast in the meantime. The public phone was already tapped and connected to a tape-recorder in a van outside. He also had a lead with earphones connected close to the hand-set so that he could listen in by Joan's side.

All that was needed now was the call from Richard Abbott.

'And what are you going to tell him?' Shepherd said for the umpteenth time.

'That it's all clear and he can come round right away.'

Her voice was mechanical and listless.

'And no tricks.'

The Betts woman smiled at her and gripped her upper arm.

'I bet you bruise easily,' she said.

Joan felt the bony fingers tightening, and again that feeling of helplessness came over her. A tear ran down her cheek.

'Ah now, don't cry,' said Betts, delicately wiping the tear away with the corner of a small handkerchief. 'We don't want you sounding upset when he rings, do we?' She smiled again till her eyes disappeared. 'Besides, we haven't given you anything to cry about . . . yet.'

After they had waited more than an hour the phone rang.

Joan picked up the receiver and said, 'Garfield Court.'

'Joan?' It was Richard.

'Yes?'

'All clear?'

'All clear. You can come round right away.'

'Good, I'll be along.'

'Ask him where he's ringing from,' Shepherd whispered to her.

'Where are you ringing from?'

There was a moment's hesitation. 'The Savoy. . . . Why do you ask?'

'Just wondered.'

'Ask him how long he'll be.'

'How long will you be, darling?'

'I'm not sure. Soon. I've a couple of things to see to first.' There was silence on the line. Then he said. 'Joan, you've been wonderful. Thanks for everything.'

And hung up.

'Right,' said Shepherd, 'let's go up to the flat and prepare our little reception party.'

He crossed to the lift followed by Betts and Joan and three Special Branch men. Betts never let go of Joan.

A notice on the lift said it was meant for four persons only and two of the Special Branch men said they would walk up, but Betts said, 'We can all squeeze in,' and herded Joan into a corner and pushed up against her. Joan thought she would suffocate.

'You're a good girl,' said Shepherd.

'Hear that?' said Betts, putting a hand under Joan's chin and lifting her head. 'You're a good girl.'

Then Shepherd said to Betts: 'I nearly pissed myself when he said, "Joan, you've been wonderful. Thanks for everything." '

Abbott came out of the Piccadilly Hotel into the evening sunshine and turned towards the Circus. Now he had another problem.

Eros didn't look the same. Nor did the Circus. But they were always mucking it about. And the girls – why were they all wearing what looked like surgical boots? Of course, fashions always change every couple of years or so. . . . Your mind is wandering, he told himself. Concentrate. On your problems preferably. Of which you have enough. But first find the whore who's made a hit with Njala.

Following the instructions of Kotiadis he had no difficulty finding the pub, which was round the corner in Brewer Street, or the big dark smiling Doris.

She was big all right. Or perhaps generous would be more accurate. There was a lot of her but most of it was in the right place.

'Are you Doris?'

'Who are you, dear?'

She had an amiable voice, with more than a hint of Cockney in it.

'Well, I'm not exactly a friend of Mr Osborn's. . . .'

'That frog-eyed fart's got no friends, dear.'

'Do you want to make some bread? Some real bread?'

'How?' She was immediately suspicious.

Abbott nodded towards a table in the corner.

'Let's sit down over there and have a drink, and I'll explain.'

'What are you?'

'An agent.'

'For what?'

'For anything I can get ten per cent of.'

'Listen, dear,' she said in that amiable voice, 'I already got a ponce, and he'd beat the shit out of you.'

'You listen, dear,' Abbott said just as amiably. 'I've never seen the ponce I couldn't punch a hole in. So let's not talk about ponces, eh? Let's talk business.'

Doris studied him. She was a judge of men, she had to be. And he was harder than he looked, she decided, a lot harder. She smiled.

'Okay,' she said. 'What's your name?'

'George Wilson.'

Abbott bought drinks and they sat at the corner table. He explained that he was an agent for English, Continental and American sex magazines. And they would be very interested in a story about President Njala.

'One Night of Love with a Cock-happy Nig-nog? That sort of thing?'

'Something like that.'

'Look, if I started telling tales out of school—'

'It would all be done under an assumed name – you know, by Josephine Entretenue—'

'Who?'

'Or Jane Shore or Fanny Hill or whatever you like.'

'Who'd do the writing? I can't hardly write a letter home to Mum.'

'You leave all that to me.'

'How much is it going to be worth?'

'A monkey. Maybe a grand. Depends on what you can remember.'

Doris was still doubtful. 'To tell you the truth I don't remember much about him – except that he never stops screwing. Last time I was stoned out of me head.'

'Don't worry; we'll start with the next time. You remember all you can. And I don't mean just sex, but all the little details people like to know – what he has for breakfast, all the security precautions and so on. I bet they search you when you go in.'

'Blimey, they look everywhere except up me you-know-what. Can I have another drink?'

Frank Smith was puzzled. He had been trying to get hold of Shepherd to tell him of his encounter with Abbott. But Shepherd couldn't be found. Smith phoned his office, who said Shepherd was out of town. They didn't know where he'd gone or when he would be back.

Smith assumed he'd gone to Petersfield to look over the safe house. But when he phoned the house Shepherd wasn't there either and wasn't expected.

It was unlike Shepherd to go swanning off without saying where he could be contacted. He was meticulous about that sort of thing. Not clever, but meticulous.

Then Smith remembered and went cold. Of course. Joan. That's why he hadn't wanted anyone to be able to get hold of him – least of all Smith.

He reached for the phone. But before he could pick it up it rang. And it was Shepherd.

'I've got him.' The voice was hoarse with triumph.

'Abbott? You've actually got him?'

'It's in the bag. He's coming here.'

'Where?'

'His ex-wife's place. That's where he spent the night. And where he'll be within the next hour or so. And where we're waiting for him – with a full reception committee.'

'What have you done to her?'

'Who?'

'You know who. Joan.'

'Interrogated her, that's all. And she coughed the lot. Very helpful she was. Still is.'

'You bastard.'

'What did you say?'

Frank Smith chose his words carefully, not wishing to say anything he might later regret. 'You fucking bastard,' he said slowly and put the phone down and went out into Queen's Gate and caught a taxi.

After a few drinks Doris got sentimental about the past. She smiled tenderly, her eyes hazy with reminiscence.

'Talking about ponces,' she said, which they weren't, 'I had a smashing ponce when I was fifteen.'

Then, as two football fans came in in tartan trews and tam-o'-shanters with Scotch favours pinned to their coats, she said, 'Jesus, Huckey McTuckles.'

'Who?'

'The Scotch. Up for the match.'

'Why do you call them Huckey McTuckles?'

'It's the way they talk. You want to get out of this place before it fills up with 'em. If they've won, they'll get pissed and awkward, if they've lost they'll get even more pissed and awkward. They're the rough trade. Some girls don't mind but I won't go near 'em. Now when the Welsh come to Twickenham that's different. All they want to do is drink and sing and have a woman. And if they win – and they usually do, thank God – it's a whores' gala west of Holborn.'

But Abbott wasn't really listening any more, he was concentrating on his next problem, which seemed insoluble.

Frank Smith held her in his arms. She was sobbing and trembling. She had run to him as soon as he walked in. He held her very tight and the realisation came to him that he loved her and had probably loved her for a long time. It didn't burst on him like a revelation, it was merely another awareness that had gently surfaced from the dark.

'If you knew what they did. If you *knew*. . . .'

He didn't need telling. He hushed and comforted her like a fretful child.

'Don't cry,' he said softly. 'Don't give this scum the satisfaction.'

To his surprise the sobbing quietened, then stopped.

'I'm taking you back with me,' he said. 'Go and pack a bag.'

She went into the bedroom, leaving him with Shepherd, Betts and the three Special Branch men.

He meant to control himself rigidly, but a spasm of anger shook him, then caught his throat so that he couldn't speak. Something throbbed in his temple. He saw a heavy bronze figurine on a side-table and wondered if he'd have time to smash it into Shepherd's face before the Special Branch men could stop him. He'd never thought himself capable of murder.

His voice came back and he said, 'I'll have you for this – you and that creature.'

Shepherd smiled his lop-sided smile. 'When we've got Abbott nobody'll give a damn how we did it.'

'When you've got him. When.'

'It's a formality.' Shepherd jerked his thumb towards the bedroom. 'And *she* helped to trap him. Told him the coast was clear, told him to come round right away.'

'Told him *what?*'

'To come round right away.'

Smith gave a sudden laugh.

'You don't believe me? Well, laugh this off.'

Shepherd switched on a portable tape-recorder and played back the telephone conversation between Joan and Abbott.

'There. What about that?'

'Amazing,' said Smith, 'truly amazing. I'd never have believed it.'

And laughed again. Then he saw Joan standing in the bedroom doorway, staring at him.

In the taxi on the way back to Queen's Gate she seemed numb. He wondered if she was suffering from shock and kept his arm round her. After a time she recovered and even smiled at him.

Then she said, 'What were you laughing at in the flat?'

'A funny story I remembered.'

'A funny story?'

'Very funny. It'd kill Shepherd.'

She sat up and looked at him.

'You know something, don't you?'

'I know a funny story. About the SOE.'

'The what?'

'Special Operations Executive. During the war I helped them organise an escape route for Allied airmen shot down in Occupied France. We passed them along through a series of safe houses to the Swiss or Spanish borders. Now sometimes the Gestapo would find out about one of these houses – and just sit there waiting for the next batch of arrivals.'

'This doesn't sound like a funny story.'

'So in order to protect them we invented a marvellously simple code. You just said the exact opposite of what you meant.'

'I don't think I follow.'

'I think you do. But let me give you an example. The rule for approaching a safe house was this: you'd ring up as if you were an old friend and ask if it was all right to come round. And if the person at the other end said, Sure, come round right away, or words to that effect, you knew the Gestapo were there, breathing down their necks.'

There was a long silence.

'Don't you think that's funny? '

'Richard,' she said, 'wasn't in the war. He wasn't old enough.'

'I know, but I was. And here's the comic bit. I told him about that code.'

He didn't know how it started. Probably someone said something someone else didn't like. That was how those things usually started.

Doris had left, and he was about to leave himself when the bar seemed to explode into violence. At the centre of it was a mob of Huckey McTuckles whose effect was that of a whirlpool. They sucked everybody into their violence.

Abbott made for the door. The last thing he wanted to get mixed up in was a fight – or anything else likely to draw the attention of the police.

He edged carefully round the boiling mob, ignoring the occasional stray punch, including one that caught him full in the mouth. He almost made it to the door when a man who'd had a broken glass jabbed in his face and was blinded by blood stumbled into him. Abbott shoved him aside, but the man tripped and fell, grabbed at Abbott and dragged him down.

Then an enormous Scotchman jumped on him, sat on his chest, grabbed his hair and started banging his head on the floor. Abbott reached down, found a clump of genitals and squeezed. The man let out a gibbering moan and fell back, half-fainting with pain.

As Abbott got to his feet more Huckey McTuckles were pouring through the door, swearing and shrieking with excitement, their built-in radar leading them infallibly to trouble. Behind them came the police.

There was no way out, so one had to be made – or he'd be arrested with the others.

He picked up a table, threw it through a big old-fashioned

window and went out after it – straight into a policeman, who spun him expertly round and twisted his arm up behind his back. Abbott relaxed then stabbed his heel backwards at the man's knee-cap in a karate kick. The policeman grunted and went down. Another policeman reached for him and Abbott grabbed his arms, pulled him forward and sideways and swept his front foot from under him. Then he ran.

He found himself in Lexington Street, ran across Broadwick Street into Poland Street, then slowed to a walk to catch his breath. At the corner of Great Marlborough Street he picked up a taxi – and gave the first address that came into his head.

As he lay back in the cab he realised he was bleeding. His mouth was cut and bleeding from a punch and there was a gash three or four inches long in his left forearm. He must have caught it on a piece of glass as he went through the pub window. It had ripped open his sleeve, which was soaked in blood from wrist to elbow. Lucky it had missed the artery.

He tried to sit up but felt dizzy from loss of blood. He lay back again and took several deep breaths and the dizziness passed. If only the bloody arm would stop bleeding.

There was a saying they had in the RAF when things went wrong. And things had certainly gone wrong. He had no shelter and no money – apart from a few pounds. Enough perhaps for a night in a cheap hotel. But he could hardly walk into a hotel with a gashed arm, a bruised and bleeding face and no luggage.

He looked out of the window. And now it was starting to rain.

'Hooray fuck,' he said.

'Beg pardon?' said the cab-driver.

'Just an old saying,' said Abbott.

When he paid the cab off at the corner of Portobello Road the cabbie got a good look at him for the first time.

'Gawd, you bin in the wars, guv '

He walked down Chepstow Villas, then saw a policeman coming towards him. To avoid another close-up inspection he started to cross the road, but the dizziness overtook him again. He swayed, stumbled on the kerb and fell.

The policeman ran to him and helped him to his feet. He was a youngster, not more than twenty-five.

'You all right, sir?' Then, after a closer look : 'What happened to you?'

'Well, officer, you see that house over there. . . .'

He pointed over the policeman's shoulder. As the policeman turned to look, Abbott ran.

He could have threatened him with the gun of course, but British police, especially the younger ones, are notorious for ignoring guns, and it was no part of his plan to shoot down innocent policemen.

So he ran. He could hear the policeman running after him, and he could feel his strength ebbing.

Only desperation kept him going.

He waited till they were chained together. He also waited till the guard sat down in the shade of a thorn-tree to eat his lunch.

Prisoners worked in pairs felling trees and in gangs of twenty under the eye of a guard. Each pair was chained together at the ankle. The guard picked the pairs at random, making sure the same two men were never chained together on consecutive days. Sooner or later though he would be chained to Kirote. It was simply a question of waiting.

He watched the guard eating with the total concentration of an animal.

His heart began to thump and he breathed deeply and evenly several times to calm himself. Then he turned to Kirote and shouted, 'You black bastard!' Kirote hit him in the face and he went down as if pole-axed.

He kept his eyes closed and heard the guard lumber over and say something to Kirote in the vernacular. He waited for and heard the whip whistling through the air. His whole body seemed to leap as it bit into him. He managed to stay still and silent – he was supposed to be unconscious. He heard the guard cursing and felt himself cringe. Another blow of the whip might tear a scream out of him before he could bite it back.

He opened his eyes fractionally, squinting through his lashes, and saw the guard bend down and unlock the shackle round his ankle.

As soon as he straightened up and turned to say something to Kirote, Abbott swung his legs in a scything action, sweeping the guard's legs from under him.

He went down on his back. Kirote dropped heavily on to him, kneeing him in the belly. As his head came up in a reflex action, he slashed the edge of his hand across his windpipe, smashing the thyroid cartilage, precisely as Abbott had taught him.

They took the guard's gun, knife, keys and water-bottle. Abbott kept the gun, a Combat Magnum, gave the knife to Kirote and threw the keys to the nearest of the other prisoners.

'Tell them they'll all get blamed for this,' he said to Kirote.

When the hunt started it would be better if they were hunting twenty men than just two. Better for the two, that is.

12

ALICE decided to get her washing and other chores done early because a girl called Philippa, who also worked in the Department, would be coming round for coffee later in the evening.

Immediately after dinner Alice washed her hair and treated it with a special conditioner guaranteed to leave it silky shiny and tangle-free, and to add a lustre irresistible to men.

Then she washed her smalls and hung them on a line over the bath. She changed Solomon's water, topped up his feeding-bowl and gave him a new sanded sheet for the bottom of the cage. She had taken him to the vet, to find out why he wouldn't sing. But the vet could find nothing wrong with him and said it was probably a mood and would pass.

She put on a clean blouse and skirt and combed out her hair. She decided it looked nice, which it did, and that the conditioner greatly improved it, which it did not.

Finally she whisked round the flat and tidied it up. She didn't want that cow Philippa, with her sharp eyes, sharp nose and sharp tongue, making snide remarks to the girls at the office ('You should *see* the place, my dear: slut's paradise. . . .').

Philippa was a horsey girl from the shires, always talking about hunt balls and point-to-points (Alice wasn't even sure what a point-to-point was, but didn't want to reveal the depths of her ignorance by asking). Her other interest was men, whom she pursued with the relentlessness if not the success she pursued foxes with.

Alice, who didn't like her but was soft-hearted, invited her round because Philippa was suffering the effects of a punctured romance, her latest young man having jilted her (for a horse, according to an unkind story going round the office).

Alice had just put the kettle on for coffee when the door-bell rang. She sighed, beginning to regret the invitation.

The bell rang again. And went on ringing.

'All right, *coming*,' Alice called out irritably, and went into the tiny entrance hall not much bigger than a cupboard.

'Really!' she said, pulling open the door.

Richard Abbott, ashen-faced and gasping for breath, his eyes closed, was leaning against the bell. Blood dripped from his left sleeve on to the mat. He almost fell against her.

'Richard,' she said. 'Richard. . . .'

He opened his eyes.

'Can I . . . rest a bit?'

He swayed.

'Dizzy,' he said.

She put her arms round him, supported him and led him into the sitting-room. He was soaking wet from sweat and rain and leaned heavily on her.

He's ruining my clean blouse, she thought inconsequently She was confused and a little frightened and seemed to have no control of her thoughts or emotions. But underneath it all she was happy. That was the one clear positive emotion she could identify. She was happy and she knew it. She could feel the love she had held down for two years rising in her like the rising sun, filling her with a warmth and tenderness that almost hurt. She could have cried with happiness. Cry later, she told herself.

She got him into an armchair and he lay back and closed his eyes again. His breathing was easier and the colour was coming back into his face, but he had begun to shiver.

She got a brightly-coloured mohair car-rug her mother had given her for Christmas and put it round his shoulders. Then she remembered the kettle which was boiling its head off. She ran into the kitchen and quickly made a hot lemon drink with plenty of sugar and a tot of whisky.

'Here you are – whisky and lemon.'

He took a sip.

'How do you feel?'

'A lot better.'

'What happened?'

'Got mixed up in a scrap. With some football fans.'

'When you've had the drink we'll clean you up and have a look at that arm.'

'I think it's stopped bleeding.'

'How did you do it?'

'Went through a window – trying to avoid the police.'

'It'll probably need stitching. And you'd better get out of those wet clothes'

She helped him get his coat off, then saw the shoulder-holster and gun swelling under his armpit like a growth. The whole thing looked evil and ugly and reminded her of those American films where detectives and other thugs walk around in shirtsleeves with their shoulder-holsters on display.

She took it off and hung it over the back of a chair. Its heaviness surprised her.

Then she helped him out of the rest of his clothes and spread them on a night-storage heater to dry. She wrapped him in more blankets to keep him warm while she washed and dressed the wound in his arm, for which she made a sling. It still bled intermittently.

'You should've been a nurse.'

'I was – for two years. Sometimes I wish I'd stuck to it.' Then, as an afterthought : 'No I don't.'

'What do you mean?'

'If I'd stayed a nurse I wouldn't've met you.'

He looked at her and she lowered her head in the way she had, suddenly shy. And he realised that when he was lying there in the chair exhausted she could have phoned the police – it was her clear duty – and that the thought had never entered her head.

He reached out and ran his hand through her hair.

'You're a good girl,' he said.

'That arm needs stitching or it'll never stop bleeding,' she said, keeping her head lowered. 'There's a hospital at the top of Ladbroke Grove. We'll get a cab there when your clothes are dry.'

She knew he was still looking at her and she went into the kitchen and made tea.

'When did you last eat?'

'I had some toast for breakfast.'

'And nothing since?'

'I'm not hungry.'

'But you must have something.'

'I spent two years on a small diet. My stomach grew small to accommodate it.'

'You're not thin though.'

'Efficient metabolism. Low fuel consumption, high energy output.'

'Please, Richard, have something. A piece of toast.'

'All right, a piece of toast.'

She made a thick piece of toast, plastered it with butter and watched with satisfaction as he ate it.

'There,' she said. 'Feeling better?'

'No,' he said. 'Feeling just the same.'

He smiled and she thought how nice he looked when he smiled. As a rule his face was on the sad side. Or perhaps it was just his eyes.

The door-bell rang. She jumped up.

'Oh my God, bloody Philippa.'

'Who?'

'Philippa Page. The horsey one in Transport.'

'Very appropriate.'

'I'll get rid of her.'

She went quickly to the front door and opened it.

'Philippa, I'm awfully sorry. I've got the most terrible curse—'

'Haven't we all, darling. Time of the month.' Philippa threw back her head, gave her neighing laugh and made to enter. Alice barred the way.

'I really do feel awful. Splitting headache and all the rest of it.'

'I'll make you a nice cup of tea. Then take two aspirins—'

'I'm sorry, I just can't face company tonight.'

She was flustered, she wasn't used to lying. Philippa looked at her with frowning suspicion.

'What *is* the matter, darling?'

'I told you, this frightful curse.'

'Oh, come off it, darling. Who cares about a bit of dysmen? There's something else, isn't there?'

She tried to look past Alice into the flat, but Alice leaned across and blocked the view.

'What *is* it?'

Alice blushed, lowered her head.

'Nothing.'

Phillippa stared at her. 'You've got a man in there.'

The tone was accusing, almost Victorian. Alice lifted her head and stared back.

'Yes I have – if it's any bloody business of yours.'

Philippa gave a little 'Oh' of astonishment and Alice shut the door in her face.

'There. Silly nosey cow,' she said going back into the sitting-room.

'You're upset,' said Abbott.

'No I'm not.'

Abbott studied her flushed face and agitated manner.

'It's just that I don't like lying. And being rude.'

'Even to a silly nosey cow?'

He smiled at her and she felt better and smiled back.

'It'll be all over Transport tomorrow you've taken a lover.'

'Tomorrow's Saturday. Let's get you to hospital.'

She rang for a mini-cab, then helped him dress.

'Those scars on your back. . . .'

'Njala's police.'

At the hospital a cool young Indian casualty-officer sutured the arm and asked in precisely accented English how it happened.

'I got mixed up with some drunken football fans.'

'A not uncommon occurrence, I fear. Did one of them cut you with a knife?'

'No. I got shoved around a bit and put my hand through a window.'

'Football arouses strange passions. But then other people's tribal customs always seem strange. The arm should not be subjected to strain or exertion for a few days. . . .'

Alice had asked the cab to wait, and on the way home, sitting there in the dark with his arm round her, lit by flickers of light from the disappearing street-lamps, she wished they could drive on forever like this, on and on forever, right off the edge of the world into silence and starlight.

'I get absurd ideas sometimes,' she said.

He didn't say anything, but as the cab drew up outside the flat he leaned forward and said to the driver, 'Take us on for a bit, will you? Round Hyde Park.'

'Christ,' she said, 'you must be psychic.'

When they got back she ran a bath for him.

'It'll be awkward with this arm.'

'I'll give you a hand.'

She liked him being a bit helpless and needing her.

It was only when he stepped out of the bath and she was drying him that she suddenly became aware of his body, and stopped.

He lifted her head and looked into her eyes.

'Don't be shy,' he said.

'I'm not really,' she said. 'I'm just not used to . . . being with a man.'

And went on drying him.

He ran his hand through her hair.

'I like your hair,' he said, and picked up his clothes. 'You've been marvellous. You've given me a real break. A real rest.'

He started to dress.

'What are you doing?'

'Getting dressed.'

'Dressed? But you're not going out?'

'No?'

'But you can't go out,' she said, saying the first thing that came into her mind. 'It's . . . it's raining.'

He sat sown on the edge of the bath and started to laugh.

'I'm too delicate to go out in the rain?'

'But aren't you . . . going to stay here?'

He stood up, put his hands on her shoulders. 'I'd like to. Of course I'd like to but. . . .' He sighed. 'Do you know what you might be letting yourself in for?'

'No,' she said with a passion that surprised her, 'I don't know and I don't bloody care.'

'If the Department were to find out. . . .'

'How the hell could they? Unless I told them. And I'm hardly likely to do that, am I?'

He waited a moment, watching her carefully.

'Aren't you? In the cold light of dawn – when you've had a chance to think things over?'

'Christ, don't you know?'

'What?'

'How I feel. Like I felt two years ago. Only worse. Or better.' She sniffed.

'Don't cry.'

'I'm not crying, I'm sniffing.'

He felt constrained by the emotionalism he had aroused – and was exploiting.

'It's all right, then, if I stay a couple of days?'

'It's all right with me if you stay for ever.' He hair had fallen across her face and she drew it back behind her ears. 'I know you think you're exploiting me – because you can't help it. You've no choice. But I'm doing what I'm doing because I want to. And you don't have to love me in return or anything. Or even pretend to. . . . So you see, you're not exploiting me at all.'

She believed instinctively that opportunities for happiness, however short-lived, should be taken. Anyway, it was in the nature of happiness to be short-lived.

In bed later she said, 'Please keep still a moment. I want to try and remember this. I tried to once before but couldn't.'

She wanted to fix it in her mind forever : this one moment, the particular sensation, the smell of him, the feel of him, the sight of him bulking over her in the dark like a big black shadow but solid and alive and beautiful.

'Christ, you're beautiful,' she said and moved against him.

'Kiss me,' she said. 'With the kisses of your mouth.'

She knew she'd never remember, but she didn't care any more.

Frank Smith was dreaming. He had put Joan up in the spare room but now in his dream she was standing by his bed. Dreams are always crazy of course. Then he woke up and found she was standing by his bed. It was ridiculous.

'This is ridiculous,' he said.

'What do you want for breakfast.'

'I cook my own breakfast.'

'Not while I'm here.'

'This is ridiculous,' he said again. 'Do you really want to know?'

'Yes.'

He told her.

'Thank you,' she said and climbed into bed beside him.

'What are you doing?'

'To hell with the spare room,' she said. 'I'm lonely.'

'Well,' he said, delighted but trying not to show it. 'Well....'

He felt inadequate but she soon altered that.

The Controller was not sleeping but staring up into the darkness worrying.

He had a great deal to worry about. He was the only one, apart from Frank Smith, who appreciated what he was up against.

He felt restless and kept changing his positions but did it slowly and surreptitiously for fear of disturbing his wife and setting off one of those kicking spasms. What a life for a cultured man.

The Minister spent the evening at the theatre watching a sex-comedy he found as sexy as toothache and just about as funny

The black girl, who was in it, had been asking him to go for months and finally, having run out of excuses, he went. The only bits he liked were when she was posturing on stage and he was remembering the posturing they did together off stage.

'Great show,' he told her afterwards. 'Marvellous.'

'And how was I?'

'Terrific. What a range. Like a black Bernhardt.'

'Are you pulling my leg?'

'Of course not. I mean it. Sincerely.'

Then he took her back to the flat in Fulham. Afterwards, driving home in a satisfied day-dream, he carelessly drove past the Royal Marsden, which he normally avoided. It looked big and bleak rising up above the street-lights into darkness. And he had a vision of his wife, pale-faced and sweating, quietly dying by inches up there in that flower-filled room.

He turned the car radio on loud.

Later in the night when he was asleep Alice leaned on her elbow and looked down at him in the moonlight reflected from the white-painted wall outside her bedroom window.

Very gently she pulled back the covers and even more gently rubbed her hand across his bare chest. It seemed more sensual and more loving than anything she had done before. He breathed deeply and regularly, his sleep undisturbed. She went on rubbing his chest and staring down at him or what she could see of him in the reflected moonlight.

13

IN THE early hours of the morning Modibo Njala was packing – or rather, Arthur was packing and Njala moodily
watching.

He was without a woman for once and it put an edge on his
already unstable temper. The intelligent Arthur was more
self-effacing than ever.

Njala wandered restlessly round the penthouse, the heaviness in his genitals irritating him like an itch, and out on to
the terrace. He looked at Hyde Park in the moonlight and
the midget figures of men and women in Park Lane climbing
into cars and taxis. Once or twice he fancied he could hear
their laughter and it teased his imagination. He got a pair of
field-glasses to see the women better, but the angle and the
height made it difficult to get more than a glimpse of curves
undulating through a patch of light till the darkness cheated
him again.

He went back inside.

'That bloody country house. The idea appals me. Ring that
man Smith and tell him I've changed my mind. I'm not going.'

'Yes, sir.'

'No – I'll phone him myself. What's the time?'

'Half-past two, sir.'

'I hate women. Did you know that, Arthur? I hate them.'

'No, sir,' said Arthur, 'I didn't know that.'

He went on packing. Njala wandered again, stopping by a
pile of books.

'Are these the ones we're taking with us?'

'If you approve, sir.'

'Montaigne. Yes, I like him, he's got a dirty mind. Yes,
and Oblomov. We're all lazy at heart.'

He picked up another book. '*A Month in the Country?*

You're not trying to be funny, I hope, Arthur? Anyway, we've got one Russian, and one Russian's enough. . . . Strange, first they want to kill me, now they want to save me.'

Arthur looked at him blankly.

'The English, Arthur, I'm talking about the English.'

'You really believe they sent that man to kill you?'

Njala shrugged. 'There's no proof. But looking at all the circumstances I should think it's highly likely.'

'I didn't know they went in for that kind of thing.'

'Oh yes they do – if the price is right. They're pirates. Always have been. It's a tradition, like poetry. Their greatest gifts – piracy and poetry. Now in decline, of course, like everything else. But just because they're no longer swarming up the rigging with a knife in their teeth doesn't mean they've forgotten how to kill.'

He stared out of the window, lost in thought. It had started raining again.

'I bet it'll be draughty and damp. Or the heating's off and no one knows how to turn it on.'

With a violent movement that made Arthur jump he swept the pile of books off the table.

'I want a woman,' he said.

Alice was awake early. She woke from a deep sleep, drowsy and warm and happy, feeling Abbott's back against her. He was still asleep. She eased herself gently out of bed, careful not to wake him, looked at her naked reflection in a wall-mirror and smiled, yawned, brushed her hair and finally put on a dressing-gown.

She went down to the front door to fetch the milk. It was going to be warm again. The sun was out but had not yet dried the overnight rain, and the streets were still damp and fresh. She took a deep breath and smiled at the milkman, who was delivering next door. She felt like smiling at everyone. She also felt she must be aware of every moment before it disappeared.

She ran upstairs and put the kettle on, then uncovered Solomon.

'Why don't you sing, you stupid bird? That famous song. His left hand is under my head, his right hand caresseth me. . . .'

Solomon stayed silent.

She made tea and took a cup into the bedroom. As she put it on the bedside table she saw he was awake and looking at her.

He sat up and opened the dressing-gown and started kissing her thighs and belly.

'Richard,' she said, her voice not quite steady. 'Richard, if you don't stop I think I'll melt.'

He pulled her into bed.

'The tea,' she said. 'The tea'll get cold.'

Later, when they were having breakfast in the big living-room, sitting by the window in the early sunlight that always seems so yellow, talking idly over coffee and toast, she had a feeling of unreality that often comes with happiness.

She tried to impress certain details on her mind as a mnemonic : a darn in the white tablecloth where his hand was resting, the button missing from his shirt, the careless way the sleeves were rolled up about his wrists, the way the veins stood out on the back of his hands, the dark stubble on his chin, the way one of his eyelids drooped slightly. . . . She thought that if she could recall the details she would be able to recall the whole scene and the feelings that went with it and warmed her like that yellow sun.

'It's nice here. A nice place. I remember. . . .'

'What?'

'We used to come back here for coffee after I'd taken you to dinner.'

She nodded. 'Coffee at my place. Always my place. Until the night you took me to your place.'

'You still make jam? Is this yours?' He pointed to a small pot on the table.

'Yes.'

'How *is* the office?'

'Occupied with politics and fornication as usual.'

'How's old whatsisname? Chap who used to run Maintenance.'

'Edwards? Retired. It's Pilkington now.'

'I know, the one that drinks. And what about the chap in Accounts with the funny name – Gimbel? Mean bastard. Never pass your expenses.'

'Oh, he's still around.'

She stopped, looked at him.

'What you want to know for? They weren't your friends.'

'I had dealings with them. And I just' – he shrugged – 'wondered.'

She was sharper than he thought. He decided to change the subject.

'Are you going out this morning? Shopping or anything?'

'I thought I'd get you some clothes. You've got to have a new jacket for a start. And I thought I'd get a couple of shirts, some socks and a pair of slacks. Oh, and a dressing-gown.'

He looked at his torn and blood-stained jacket.

'That's had it, I suppose. But there's no need to waste your money on anything else.'

'I *want* to buy you something. It would give me pleasure.'

'Want me to come with you?'

'Why take the risk? We must have hundreds of people out looking for you.'

'And you're the one who's found me.'

'I've been looking the longest. . . . All my life.'

'Alice,' he said after a moment, 'you know I can't stay long.'

He didn't want her to get ideas.

'How long is long?'

'I don't know. Two days, three days. . . .'

'They say time's not important, it's what you do with it. But when time's all you've got, when a few hours is all you've got to last you a lifetime maybe. . . . Anyway, it's psychological, isn't it?'

'What?'

'Time. It goes fast when you're happy, slow when you're

sad. Everyone knows that. So I'm not going to be sad worrying about the future. When I don't want to think about something I . . . just don't think about it. I know it's childish but that's how I exist.'

'It's how most people exist.'

'But not you.'

'Me too.'

'But that's ducking reality, isn't it?'

She drew her hair back and curved it smoothly behind her ears in that characteristic gesture, revealing her earnest young face and the shadowy division of her breasts as the dressing-gown opened a little.

'But then what *is* real? Whenever I feel happy I wonder if it's real.'

He slipped his hand in the opening of the gown and cupped one of her breasts, brushing the nipple gently with his thumb.

'That's real,' she said. 'Christ, that's real all right.'

She stayed still with the relaxed stillness of an animal and he went on gently caressing her. She had released a sensuality in him he didn't know he possessed.

'This is crazy,' he said.

'No, it isn't,' she said, 'it's sane. The only sanity maybe.'

Njala breakfasted alone as usual while the woman they had found for him at three o'clock in the morning slept on.

He felt full of life and vigour as he worked his way through an enormous breakfast, glanced at the morning papers and read with care reports from his chief of police about suspected and even possible political opponents.

Frank Smith had breakfast with Joan. It was an odd experience to have breakfast with someone, to have it cooked for him and be waited on.

He wondered what to say.

'You had no difficulty in, er, finding things then?'

'Frank,' she said, 'I'm not used to talking at breakfast either. So why, don't you just carry on as usual and read your paper?'

While he watched her dressing Abbott asked her if she knew anything about the precautions to safeguard Njala.

'No,' Alice said. 'And you could hardly expect me to tell you if I did.'

She pulled on a pair of tights, smoothing them carefully over her thighs with both hands and making sure they fitted under the crotch.

'They know you've found out about his hotel though. And they'd like to move him somewhere else. The last I heard he was being difficult.'

She examined herself critically in the wall-mirror to see if the tights fitted properly. Then she put on a bra, blouse and skirt.

'I'm getting fat,' she said after a final inspection.

'You're not.'

She held her head sideways, put a clip in her mouth and started brushing her hair, which was long and brown and had coppery tints.

'Shepherd,' she said indistinctly through her teeth, 'thinks you're mad. So do I.'

Shepherd. So that was the bastard breathing down Joan's neck when he phoned. Yes, he remembered Shepherd and his methods of interrogation.

He looked at his watch. 'I'm going out.'

She wanted to argue, warn him, persuade him, but what was the point?

'Do you want to take the car?'

She pointed out of the window to a little Fiat 500 parked nearby.

'Florence.'

'Florence?'

'Yes, it's rather old-fashioned, but she's a rather old-fashioned lady. Florence Fiat.'

'Thanks, but I don't think I'll need a car.'

'Will you be long?'

'I shouldn't think so. An hour perhaps.'

'Please, Richard, take care, won't you?'

After he had gone she sat and stared at the phone. She had

an overwhelming desire to phone Frank Smith and tell him everything. It would certainly save Njala's life and probably Richard's too – which was a lot more important.

Though it was Saturday morning and not yet nine, traffic was heavy as Abbott walked up Park Lane. He stopped outside Njala's hotel and pretended to light a cigarette while his eyes made a guarded search of the front and the foyer, which he could see through the glass doors.

Outside, talking to a fat and uniformed commissionaire was a tall, broad-shouldered, flat-faced young man in a conservatively cut dark-blue suit. A few yards away, leaning against a pillar of the entrance porch was a remarkably similar young man. They could have been twins except that their faces were different and the second one was wearing a grey suit. Special Branch. Picked for the speed of draw and accuracy at firing from the hip (he remembered the gunnery instructor: 'Just point and fire. If you point your forefinger you'll find it's accurate. So imagine the gun is your forefinger').

And there were two more who looked like Special Branch men in the foyer, sitting neatly and self-consciously on one of those black buttoned leather sofas you see on TV, watching everyone who came in.

Then someone came out. A girl came out, swaying, drunk (at nine in the morning? At nine in the morning).

In an unmistakably Cockney accent she said to the fat commissionaire: 'Get us a taxi, cock.'

It was a friendly enough request but the commissionaire, because of the presence of Special Branch, no doubt, was on his dignity. Besides, *that* sort should know enough to go out of the back entrance.

'Get one yourself,' he said. 'I'm talking to my friend.'

Her voice rose one whole strident octave. 'Don't you talk to me like that, you fat poof, or I'll pull the skin of your arse over your eyes.'

She swung her handbag at him. The Special Branch man, his youth and embarrassment showing, stepped in between them and held her arms.

'Now be sensible, dear, and go home.'

'Let go of me.'

She twisted away from him, trying to break his grip – and saw Abbott on the edge of the pavement.

'George,' she called out. '*George.*'

It was Doris, bloody Doris. It would be. And she was drunk all right.

For a moment he was undecided. Should he turn the other way and walk off? Or would that be even more suspicious? The young Special Branch man was already looking at him. He would have Abbott's description and would surely recognise him up close.

Abbott unbuttoned his jacket to allow a faster draw of the Combat Magnum and went up to them, grinning. An unarmed copper was one thing, a Special Branch sharpshooter was another. If he went for his gun he'd be a dead man.

'Hallo, Doris, love, what's the trouble?'

'These bleeders think they can—'

'Get her out of here, chum,' said the Special Branch man, 'before she gets nicked.'

He was looking at Abbott but not really seeing him – partly because he was embarrassed, partly because a drunken trouble-making whore was not the sort of context he readily associated Abbott with.

'Nicked?' said Doris. 'Who the bleed'n' hell's going to nick me? I'm no five-bob whore, I've just had relations with a very important person in there.'

She made a sweeping gesture towards the hotel.

'I wouldn't mind nicking you myself, you gorgeous bitch,' said Abbott. 'Nick, nick, nick. Come on.'

For some reason this amused Doris and she started to giggle. He took her by the arm and led her away. It took an effort to turn his back on the Special Branch man though. Any moment he expected something to happen, to hear the man call out, 'Just a moment, sir,' and turn and find himself looking down the barrel of a gun. He kept his right arm free as he walked away, feeling peculiarly naked. But nothing happened. He started to breathe again.

Doris hiccupped, swayed and grabbed his left arm to steady herself. He winced.

'Whatsamatter?'

He told her about the Huckey McTuckles.

'Didn't I tell you? Wherever there's trouble there's Huckey Mcbleed'n'tuckles.'

'They seem to have an instinct for it.'

'You bet — like a dung-beetle for shit. Got a fag?'

He gave her one and she tried to light it but couldn't hold the match steady. He lit it for her.

'Doris, how come you're pissed so early in the morning?'

'I'm not pissed — I'm tired. No sleep. Our nig-nog friend never stopped except to feed his face. . . . Well, maybe a tiny bit pissed. See, I had champagne for breakfast. He asked me what I wanted and I said I've always wanted champagne for breakfast. And he clapped his hands and said to the other goon, Arthur, champagne for Ermyntrude. He calls me Ermyntrude all the time.'

She vented a huge yawn.

'What about a coffee?'

'P'raps it'll wake me up.'

He took her into a coffee-bar and by the second cup she had more or less stopped yawning.

He questioned her about security arrangements at the hotel but learnt nothing he didn't know already know or couldn't have guessed.

He wondered idly — he was already bored — what Njala saw in her. Her availability at all hours probably, unless he liked getting back to the gutter — what the French call *nostalgie de la boue.*

He was wrong. Doris had been a success.

'He likes me, old whaddymacallit.'

'He does?'

'Yeah, and you know what he likes best?'

'Your conversation.'

'Me nature. He says I've got a sporting nature.'

'I'm sure you have.'

Abbott's disinterest was obvious. Mistaking it for disbelief,

Doris said : 'You think I'm a-kidding? Well, he's invited me down to his place in the country. Tomorrow night.'

Abbott had a cup of coffee halfway to his lips. He put it down carefully and slowly.

'His place in the country?'

'Yeah. And I'm being *flown* there, what's more. By helicopter.'

'Where?'

'Dunno. It's all hush-hush. Something to do with security, on account of him being so important.'

He hadn't really expected her to know. Njala wouldn't be that stupid or careless. Still, it was a help. At least he now knew something of Njala's intended movements. And there might be more to come. A lot more.

'Now listen,' he said, 'this could be big. If you actually spend a night at his country house I could sell the story all over the Continent, America, everywhere. And with the syndication rights you'd make a bomb.'

'How much is a bomb?'

'A minimum, a guaranteed minimum of five grand.'

'Jesus,' she breathed, now cold sober and wide awake. 'Five grand. . . . Jesus.'

But I'll need plenty of authentic detail of the background – what the house looks like, the number of servants and guards, the security precautions and so on.'

He paused to let it sink in.

'Every detail, Doris.'

'For five grand, baby,' said Doris, 'you'll get every detail you can think of, including the length of his big black cock. In centimetres for the Common Market.'

She shook with laughter that made the coffee-cups rattle.

After the journey in the rain-forest – the last two days a stumbling nightmare – he felt so weak and ill he wanted to lie down in the bush and die like a sick animal.

He had no memory of reaching the coast. He just found himself there one night on a road that ran beside the mangroves. He knew he must make for the port, which lay to the north. He had seen it from a hill glimmering in the brief African dusk. Or perhaps it was a mirage.

The road was metalled but uneven and in disrepair, awkward to walk on in the dark. Occasionally a car or military jeep went by, headlights blazing, and he hid behind bushes or in a ditch.

He took a bearing from the Pole Star and pushed on as quickly as he could but seemed to be slowing down all the time, walking through cotton wool like a man in a dream. The road went on forever in the moonlight before it finally bridged a shallow river and some mud-flats and he saw the moon reflected in the oily waters of the harbour.

The whole place seemed deserted. He walked through the long shadows of the ships at the wharves, the silence making him nervy. Then, from above him, on the deck of a ship, a seaman started to sing softly. A signal perhaps, for two big black bucks stepped out of the shadows in front of him. He saw a gleam of a knife but his gun was already in his hand.

'Piss off, you creeps,' he said in the vernacular, which probably surprised them more than the gun.

He walked on towards the lights of the town. Njala's town. It was on higher ground than the port and at the northern end rose steeply to a small plateau where the presidential palace was set to catch the cool winds from the sea. It was once the official residence of the British governor. After independence it was rebuilt by the new president on a grander and more lavish scale. It was rebuilt a second time by Njala, who murdered the new president, his family, friends and supporters in a military coup of brief and bloody duration. Njala turned it from a palace into a fortress, guarded night and day by picked troops.

His presence was unavoidable, inescapable. Njala Square, Njala Place, Njala Street, statues and posters of him everywhere. Even Njala T-shirts. Njala's town all right.

Kirote's town too. The shanty-town bit anyway. That was where Kirote had lived with other political exiles not important enough to jail or shoot. Until of course he became important enough to jail – and shoot.

He was looking for Kirote's sister, who was a whore and lived on the edge of shanty town.

14

SHEPHERD and two shifts of Special Branch men waited all night at the flat for Abbott.

Towards four in the morning Shepherd fell asleep on the sofa in the living-room and woke after two hours from a bad dream in which the disembodied face of Frank Smith was laughing at him. Then it changed into Abbott's face and he tried to hit it, but his arm had no strength, as if it were made of cotton wool. He woke up sweating.

One of his men brought him a coffee. But he had a sour taste in his mouth that no amount of coffee could relieve.

'He's not coming,' he said. 'The bastard's not coming.'

He left the other Special Branch men there and went home to Upper Tooting where he lived in a mid-Victorian villa overlooking the cemetery. He tried to get some more sleep, but was overtired and lay staring at the ceiling with the sour taste still in his mouth. At nine a police car took him to Holland Park for a meeting with the Controller and Frank Smith.

He reported the misadventure with Abbott and played the tape of Abbott's telephone conversation with Joan.

'I just don't understand it. She *tells* him its okay to come round, he *says* he's coming round. You heard him. I mean, he couldn't have said it plainer, could he?'

'And you waited all night?' said the Controller.

'All bloody night.' He saw Smith smiling. 'What's so bloody funny?'

He was tired and touchy, his eyes puffed and heavy from lack of sleep. He had had no breakfast and was beginning to feel hungry. He still had that sour taste in his mouth.

Smith looked relaxed and refreshed, which he was, having had a woman, a good sleep and a good breakfast. The world looked fine for once and his natural pessimism was in abeyance.

'I was smiling,' he said, 'because I'm happy.'

He was also smiling at Shepherd's discomfiture. So he'd lost a night's sleep. Serve the big fat bastard right. He was likely to lose a few more before this job was over.

'So why *didn't* he show up?'

'Perhaps,' said the Controller, 'something happened to him. Perhaps he was in an accident.'

'We should be so lucky,' Shepherd said with a grunt.

'Is it worth ringing round the hospitals?'

'No,' said Smith, 'it is not. I know the explanation. At least, I think I do. It occurred to me when I first heard the tape last night.'

'What do you mean?' said Shepherd slowly.

Smith told them about the SOE code and watched a purplish flush spread up from Shepherd's collar till it suffused his whole face. Veins stood out on his forehead and a muscle jumped in his cheek. The small slate-grey eyes seemed to go cloudy, as if iris and pupil had merged.

'Why didn't you tell me last night?' His voice sounded as if it was being strangled in his throat.

Smith smiled his most disarming smile.

'I wasn't sure if it *was* the code. Or if the message was genuine. That's the beauty of it really – you can never be sure.'

'You still could have told me.'

'And you'd still have had to wait to make absolutely sure, wouldn't you?'

'Well, I'd've. . . .' Shepherd wasn't quite sure what to say. 'I expect I'd've waited a couple of hours, left some men there and shoved off.'

'You could've done that anyway.'

'I know, but . . . well, I wanted to be in at the death. Naturally.'

You mean you wanted the honour and the bloody glory, Smith thought. The kudos and congratulations. Wanted to be the Minister's white-haired boy, the *Wunderkind* of Scotland Yard, who had captured the assassin single-handed (apart from the help of half a dozen strong-arm men who'd be forgotten when the bouquets were handed out). Supercop does it again. But Supercop was left sitting there like a lemon all night while the rest of the population were asleep or making love like civilised people.

'I'm sorry you lost a night's sleep,' he said and smiled as Shepherd's face went that funny colour again.

He was having a small revenge for Shepherd's treatment of Joan, and Shepherd knew it and could do nothing about it except swallow his sour rage and wait for an opportunity to get even with Smith. He was the kind of man who would wait for years.

'If a situation like this occurs again,' said the Controller, 'I'd like to be advised of it immediately, not when it's all over.'

Shepherd nodded, accepting the rebuke in silence. But he was now all the more determined to get Abbott, dead or alive, without anybody's help, least of all Smith's. He avoided looking at Smith who he knew was smiling.

'Now,' said the Controller, 'how far have we got with the logistics of tonight's move?'

'I've arranged for an Air Force chopper to be on stand-by at London Heliport from eight-thirty,' said Smith.

'We'll need landing-lights at the house.'

'They're being fixed up this afternoon. On one of the lawns.'

'And you're responsible for getting him to the heliport.' This to Shepherd, who nodded.

'We'll pick him up at the hotel around nine – if he doesn't keep us waiting. It shouldn't take us more than twenty minutes to get to the heliport.'

'What sort of escort are you taking?'

'Couple of police cars, one in front, one behind, plus motor-cycle outriders.'

'*Weissen Mäuse*,' said Smith.

'What?' said Shepherd.

'White mice,' said Smith. 'That's what the Germans call them.'

'Call who?'

'Motor-cycle police with white helmets.'

Stupid bloody remark, thought Shepherd. Bloody typical.

'Really?' he said politely.

'Are you travelling with him?'

Shepherd nodded again. 'Sergeant Clifford and I will be in the car with him. And in the chopper.'

'Are you taking him out of the front of the hotel or the back?' said Smith.

'We thought the back.'

'I think the front might be better,' said Smith.

Shepherd felt his anger rising but held it down. The bastard was only trying to needle him.

'Why?'

'More people about.'

'I'm sorry, I don't follow.'

'Less chance of a clear view of the target. Much greater chance of hitting an innocent bystander.'

'You really think a psychopathic killer would care?'

'We're talking about Richard Abbott, our own agent. The man we picked to assassinate Njala. We didn't call him a psychopathic killer then.'

'Well, that's what he is now.'

'Only in your stupid little mind, which puts everything into categories because it's the only way it can function.'

Smith found himself shaking with rage.

'That will do, Frank,' the Controller said.

Shepherd smiled his lop-sided smile. He had touched a nerve.

'I was forgetting,' he said, 'he's a friend of yours.'

'You're forgetting a lot of things, including what you're up against.'

'Frank,' said the Controller, 'I said that will do.' Then to Shepherd: 'From my own knowledge of Abbott I also feel he's unlikely to start shooting in a street full of people.'

'Okay,' said Shepherd, 'we'll take Njala out the front door.'

He didn't care which door they took him out of. One of the things he did care about was getting back at Frank Smith. And in some obscure way he felt he had. It was a small satisfaction but it cheered him up. He excused himself and left, smiling.

'Frank, you must try to contain your dislike of him.'

'We oughtn't to have to work with scum like that.'

'In a perfect world we wouldn't. But in a perfect world people like us wouldn't be working at all. And Shepherd does get results. Somehow.'

'Sure,' said Smith sourly, 'and who the hell cares how.'

'Frank, every country needs people like him, *has* people like him.'

'That's why the world smells so sweet.'

The Controller gave a weak smile and went on to discuss an Intelligence report about a Russian trade delegation due at London Airport that afternoon. It said that the head of the delegation would go straight from the airport to Njala's hotel for a secret meeting with him and would join the rest of the delegation later.

'And that,' said the Controller, 'is presumably why Njala refused to leave for the country right away. He wanted to wait for the Russian.'

'That's no reason. We could've flown the Russian down there. Sandwiched between a couple of birds, no doubt.'

'The meeting *is* supposed to be secret.'

'Secret my arse. Njala must know we'd find out. Anyway, where did our report come from?'

'One of the African embassies where we have a contact.'

'And where did he get it?'

'From a contact in Njala's embassy. We think it may have been a deliberate leak.'

'Exactly. Njala wants to make sure we know he's dickering with the Russians. So he can bump the oil price up.'

'I suppose so,' said the Controller.

'No,' Smith said. 'There's something phoney about this. He's waiting for something else. Or someone else. Someone he *doesn't* want us to know about.'

'Who, for instance?'

'Christ knows. He's got more fingers in more pies than Colonel Gadafi. And they're just as nasty.'

'Can you find out?'

Smith shrugged. 'I can try. But he's a tricky bastard.'

'And a treacherous one,' said the Controller, nervously gouging his ear with his little finger.

'That's what Richard Abbott says.'

'Ah yes, I was going to ask you something about Richard.'

Frank Smith had wondered whether the Controller's preamble about the Russian trade delegation was merely a roundabout way of getting back to the subject of Abbott. But why the circumlocution? The Controller would have a reason. He always had a reason, though it wasn't always easy to define.

After his encounter with Abbott, Smith had rung the Controller and reported the whole of their conversation as accurately as he could. The Controller listened without interruption and made no comment. He merely thanked Smith and rang off. But Smith had the feeling that he was going to report the conversation to one of *his* superiors – perhaps the Minister or the Prime Minister. No one knew who gave the Controller his orders.

'From what you told me,' said the Controller, 'he sounded sane enough. For all practical purposes anyway.'

Smith nodded. The Controller was still fencing.

'And since we can't get in touch with him we can't even try to persuade him to' – the Controller gestured – 'change his mind.'

'He'll never change his mind.'

'Only God and madmen never change their mind. And since he's not exactly God—'

'He's not a madman either. At least, I don't think so. Neither would you if you met him.'

'Then how do you explain his behaviour?'

'He simply has an obsession about killing Njala. But after what he's been through so would I. So would anyone.'

The Controller nodded. 'I suppose that's understandable enough. But he doesn't really believe that nonsense about our betraying him, does he? Not in his heart.'

Now we're getting warm, Smith thought.

'Oh, he believes it all right. Especially in his heart.'

'But there's no proof, as you yourself pointed out.'

'That doesn't mean it isn't true.'

'But in this instance, surely, no reasonable person would believe it's true? I mean, you wouldn't, would you?'

So that's it, Smith thought, that's the big one, that's what they really want to know. Because if I believe Abbott was betrayed, other people in the Department might start believing it. And once our agents believe we would betray them if the price is right. . . .

'It's a very difficult question for me to answer,' he said. 'You see, if I were in Abbott's place and knew what he knows I certainly would believe the Department had betrayed me.'

'No, Frank, not you, surely?' The Controller allowed a modest proportion of pain and shock to creep into his voice (he didn't want to overdo it).

'However, since I'm not in his place, I can't allow myself to think we'd betray our own man. Otherwise I'd have to resign. And walk out. And tell the whole wide world what I thought of such a stinking rotten fucking set-up.'

Smith found himself shaking with sudden anger again. He waited till he had calmed down.

'I told you it was a difficult question to answer. I feel like a Jesuit trying to justify the unjustifiable. And I can't of course. All I can do is cloud the issue with clever words – and not examine anything too deeply, especially my own conscience.'

Neither man spoke for what seemed a long time. The Controller screwed his little finger into his ear again. Then he cleared his throat, leaned on the desk and made a steeple with his fingers.

'Frank,' he said with a solemnity that made Smith immediately suspicious, 'if Richard had been betrayed from here, I would know about it if anyone did.'

'Yes,' Smith said, 'that's what I'd more or less worked out.'

'And I can assure you we did not betray him.'

He straightened up, looked Smith in the eye and said with even greater solemnity : 'I give you my word.'

The word of a fine old English gentleman, said Smith, but not out loud.

And indeed he looked like a fine old English gentleman, with his iron-grey hair, goitrous blue eyes and slightly red face. Smith could see him giving beads to the natives in exchange for their birthright. No, that wasn't fair. He was exaggerating because he was angry. He had to believe the Controller if life were to be possible.

'I believe you,' he said. Had he been a religious man he might have crossed himself, or at least his fingers.

'Still, he *was* betrayed. By someone.'

He waited but the Controller offered no comment.

Betrayed. Why didn't they say blown, which was what they usually said? The retreat into formal language was in itself a kind of betrayal. It always is.

'I'm not supposed to tell you,' said the Controller, 'but I've recommended you for promotion – as my deputy. You'll have to go before a board of course, but that's a formality since I shall be sitting on it myself.'

Smith was too surprised to say anything.

The Controller smiled. 'I think that calls for a little celebration. I propose a champagne lunch at the Savoy.'

What are we celebrating? Smith wondered. My promotion? Or the death of my conscience?

15

AFTER he had put the sleepy Doris in a taxi Abbott walked to the Cumberland Hotel and rang Joan's flat.

A man's voice answered and gave the number.

'Mrs Abbott, please.'

'Who wants her?'

'I do, of course.'

'What is the name, please?'

'Mickey Mouse, you stupid flat-foot.'

Abbott hung up, wondering what had happened to Joan. Frank Smith would know. He rang Smith's number – and got Joan.

'Joan, how are you? Are you all right?'

She started to tell him about the interrogation but found herself getting upset.

'It's all right, you don't have to say any more. I know about Shepherd and that bisexual bitch.'

'Frank's letting me stay here. He's . . . looking after me.'

'Good. He's a nice bloke. You know, I always thought he fancied you. But he's a bit shy.'

'Richard, last night I—'

She stopped.

'Joan,' he said after a moment, 'you don't owe me anything. Least of all a confession. I'm glad Frank's looking after you, I really am. Tell him that from me, will you?'

'But what about you? What about the money? I got it for you.'

'I won't need it now, I'm all right.'

'You sure? Have you got a place to stay?'

'Yes, yes. I had a bit of luck. They say you've got to get lucky sometime, don't they?'

'Have you got a woman?'

'What?'

'You've got a woman. I can tell it from your voice.'

He laughed. 'You always think I've got a woman.'

'Try not to make her unhappy. And Richard, take care.'

'I will, I will. And change my socks twice a week.'

'You're sending me up.'

'Tell Frank I'll remember Shepherd. But not in my orisons.'

He was skating over the surface of the conversation as he always did with Joan, but she knew what he meant.

'Frank spotted the code as soon as he heard the tape of our conversation.'

'So he should.'

'But he didn't tell Shepherd. He just laughed. And left Shepherd to sweat it out all night. He hates him.'

'And likes you.'

'He likes you too.'

'A man of immaculate taste. Look after yourself, Joan.'

'And you, Richard. And you.'

He hung up, then rang Njala's hotel, announced himself as the London correspondent of *Paris Match* and said he'd like to speak to Colonel Njala's press secretary. After a time Arthur came on the line and asked him in French what he wanted.

He said the magazine wanted to do a picture-feature on Njala and he would like to interview him, preferably somewhere visually interesting, like the penthouse terrace — assuming, that is, they were occupying the penthouse.

'Yes,' said Arthur, 'we're in the penthouse. When did you want to do the interview?'

'Today, if possible.'

'That's out of the question, I'm afraid. His Excellency leaves for the country tonight.'

'Perhaps I could interview him there. I wouldn't mind a trip out of town.'

'I am afraid that won't be possible. He intends to have a complete rest and will be giving no interviews.'

'He's not ill, I hope?'

'No. Merely in need of a rest.'

'Ah well, perhaps I can see him when he gets back. Where did you say he was going?'

'I'm afraid I cannot tell you that.'

Abbott hadn't thought he would, but it was worth a try.

Afterwards he strolled in the park and found a seat from where he could see the hotel, including the terrace of the penthouse suite. If Njala came to the edge of the terrace he'd get a good view of him through a three-power 'scope. But he could hardly sit there in broad daylight with a sniper's rifle across his knees.

After dark though it would be another matter. . . . He wondered what time Njala was leaving. His thoughts began to race. Was it worth getting the rifle? And even if Njala did come out on the terrace would he be able to see him in the dark? That would depend on the background lighting. If he were silhouetted it would help. Anyway, there was an image-intensifying night-sight in the gun-case.

Ideally, he'd like Njala to know he was going to die, but that was a refinement. If there was a chance to kill him he must take it. But the chance must be weighed and precautions taken. Always precautions. And first he'd have to get the rifle, which called for more precautions still.

He put his head in his hands and thought.

Two lovers passed, arms round each other, and he was unaware of them.

The girl said to the man : 'Did you see that man on the bench, thinking? You could practically *hear* him thinking. I wonder if he's a poet or a philosopher.'

But the young man was thinking of more immediate things on that warm spring day, like the bloom on her cheeks, the smell of her skin and the way her breasts moved against her blouse and altered its shape.

You've got to get lucky sometime, as Abbott had said. Even if it goes sour on you later on.

Chief Superintendent Shepherd, in his office at Scotland

Yard, got lucky around the time Abbott was sitting in Hyde Park thinking about guns and death.

The luck happened when a team from the Yard's Bomb Squad were doing a routine sweep with metal-detectors of the left-luggage offices at main-line stations. They also had dogs with them for sniffing out explosives.

There had been a bomb scare at Euston Station the night before.

At Waterloo one of the team found a case that indicated an extremely high metal content. Another expert carefully opened the case. When he saw what was in it he rang the Yard.

Sergeant Clifford was playing with his trains when the telephone rang.

Clifford, a whey-faced, pale-eyed bachelor of low sexual drive, lived with his mother and his model trains in a featureless dormitory suburb that had nothing but a good train-service to Waterloo.

'Clifford,' said Shepherd, 'do you remember the gun that was specially made for Abbott?'

Clifford's pale eyes, which usually had a dead look, flickered into momentary life.

'Remember it?' he said. 'Will I ever forget it? I helped him test it at that army range on Salisbury Plain. A one-off job based on the Armalite Fifteen and fitted with a three-power Leatherwood 'scope. And you know the muzzle velocity? Three thousand two hundred and fifty feet a second. At five hundred yards it'll go through both sides of a steel helmet and leave a hole in your head the size of a man's fist. And as for the balance and feel, I've never known a gun as sweet to handle. . . .'

He sighed like another man might sigh over a woman.

'I think we may have found the gun – at Waterloo Station. How soon can you meet me there?'

Within half an hour Sergeant Clifford had examined and identified the gun.

'That's it. No question.'

He took the component parts out of the case and assembled them. Then he field-stripped the gun and reassembled it. He did it all very quickly but with loving care.

Then he cuddled it to his shoulder and drew a bead on a bowler-hatted man crossing the concourse towards the York Road exit.

'You could kill anything with this,' he said in a slightly hushed tone, as if speaking in church. Then, with the same speed and care he broke the rifle down and put it back in its case.

'You'd better stay here in case he shows up. But keep out of sight. I'll send you some help he's never seen before, some real heavyweights.'

'Sir, with respect, he'll suss that kind out straightaway. Let's have the kind that don't have copper written all over them. Like that long-haired git – whatsisname – Peters. And Franklin, the bright one just out of Bramshill.'

'Two? That won't be enough.'

'All right then, let's have the long thin one that looks like a preacher – Ashby. That'll make four of us. Any more and we'll be falling over one another – specially as there'll be a bit of a crowd round the counter anyway. We don't want too many bloody crooks.'

Shepherd reflected, nodded slowly. 'All right.'

'And tell 'em to wear jeans or something and look scruffy.'

'We won't want them armed though?'

'No. If I'm armed that'll be enough.'

Shepherd nodded again and rubbed his chin. Clifford had his limitations, but within them he was an expert. Shepherd had great faith in him.

'We don't want the bloody public getting shot up, do we?'

Clifford's eyes flickered and went dead again. His voice became flat and curiously formal, as if delivering a prepared statement.

'The use of firearms will, of course, be avoided . . . unless forced upon us in protection of ourselves or the public.'

Shepherd went on nodding and rubbing his chin, barely listening. Clifford cleared his throat.

'On the other hand, if it's the only way of stopping him. . . .'

Shepherd's slate-grey eyes stared into Clifford's pale eyes.

'Then stop the bastard.'

Clifford almost smiled. He disliked Abbott for the simple and childish reason that someone had once said he was a better marksman than Clifford. It wasn't even true but it rankled in Clifford's limited mind.

In the car on the way back to the office Shepherd decided, after a long argument with himself, that he would not ring the Controller. After all, why should he? He wasn't officially responsible to the Controller or anyone else in SIS. Not officially. Anyway, the mechanics of making an arrest were his province, not the Controller's. So to hell with the Controller. The moment he got back to the office he rang the Controller.

'Fine, fine,' said the Controller, who was anxious to get away for a weekend's sailing on the Solent. 'Who's in charge of the operation locally?'

'Sergeant Clifford.'

'Oh.'

There was a long silence.

'I'm not sure he's the right man to be left in charge.'

'You did say you wanted Abbott stopped . . . dead, if necessary.'

'Yes, but only Abbott. It's Waterloo Station, remember, not Lod Airport.'

Abbott got back to the flat to find Alice had bought him some clothes, but he was too preoccupied to pay much attention.

'Look,' she said of a jacket. 'Donegal tweed. Nice, isn't it?'

'Very nice,' he said absently.

'Aren't you going to try it on?'

He tried it on.

'Very nice,' he said.

'Richard, are you worried about something?'

'M'm?'

'I said—'

'No, I'm not worried.'

But he was. She could sense it, and she wanted to know why. At the same time she didn't want to know. The moment she started to think about the situation it became impossible. And like most of us when faced with the impossible or the unacceptable, she turned away from it and went on acting out her own little dream, vaguely hoping that reality would never wake her up.

'I'm in love with you,' she said. 'I never knew what that meant, though I used to think I did. But I know now.'

She looked at him and lowered her head and a wing of hair fell across one side of her face. She pushed it back behind her ear in that gesture that made her look so young and earnest and vulnerable.

He reached out and rubbed his hand along the side of her neck. She leaned her head to that side, half-trapping his hand, which was warm and dry and moved gently.

The nice thing about Waterloo Station is that it never changes. It's always the same – big, echoing and dirty. They even play the same wartime music over the loud-speakers, or so it seemed to Richard Abbott when he went there to leave a case at the left-luggage office.

He had intended to put it in a locker in the Underground but he found the lockers locked and without keys, presumably to stop terrorists planting bombs in them. He wondered if the left-luggage office was also out of action. He needn't have worried. It was thriving and in the same old corner opposite platforms 1 and 2, between a row of phone booths and a gentleman's lavatory boasting some of the choicest graffiti in London.

He watched carefully but saw no attempt to check the contents of the luggage

Near the office a grey elderly porter with a grey elderly moustache was leaning on a broom, staring gloomily at nothing. Abbott got talking to him and brought the conversation round to recent bomb-scares.

'They don't seem to bother checking luggage here.'

'They're too busy most of the time. I mean, if they sodded about opening bags all day there'd be a blockage, stands to reason.'

Abbott agreed a blockage stood to reason and joined the queue at the counter. The busy clerk hardly looked at the case and within a few moments Abbott was walking away with a ticket in his hand.

That was three days ago. Now Sergeant Clifford was waiting for him to come back, waiting with the patience of a cat behind the sliding doors at one side of the office. He was well hidden from any customers but could be out on the station concourse in seconds.

He had brought with him, in its own special holster, his own special pistol, a Remington XP-100, which is more like a miniature rifle with its bolt action, centre fire and $10\frac{1}{2}$-inch barrel. With that sort of specification and barrel length it was presumably intended as a target pistol, but perhaps the designer also had assassins (for the use of) in mind since it is chambered for the .221 Fireball, a bottleneck cartridge with the highest muzzle-velocity of any pistol cartridge in the world.

It is a single-shot pistol, but Clifford had never needed more than one shot at anything, especially if it moved. His speed and accuracy in sighting a moving target were this side of phenomenal, but only just.

Outside the left-luggage office and leaning against the wall on either side of it were two young hippies. One had a wide-brimmed hat, fringed jacket and worry beads, the other had shoulder-length hair and a flower-power shirt stuffed into ragged jeans. They looked scruffy and bored, as if they had nothing better to do than hold up the wall and smoke cigarettes. They were two of the Special Branch men Sergeant Clifford had asked for.

The third, the tall thin tubercular-looking Ashby, was leaning against the back of one of a row of wooden benches opposite the luggage counter. He wore a dusty black suit and black string tie and was squinting short-sightedly at a pocket Bible. He looked like one of those Hot Gospellers come out of the Deep South to save souls with one hand and seduce women with the other.

A maintenance electrician had rigged up a buzzer under the counter for the clerk to press with his foot. That was to be the signal for Clifford and the others to go into action.

It was a simple plan and seemed foolproof. All they had to do was wait for the fish to bite, then pull him in.

The fish bit late in the afternoon when a small crowd of seven or eight people were bunched round the counter. Among them were two large and noisy drunks. The plan had allowed for a small crowd but not for large drunks.

The first four people at the counter were holding out their tickets, but the only one the clerk really saw was the ticket held by a man dressed like a tramp with a battered hat pulled down over his eyes and a long filthy overcoat. It was the ticket he had been waiting for all day. He put his foot hard on the buzzer.

The two Special Branch men on either side of the office started to shoulder through the crowd. One tried to shove the larger of the two drunks aside.

'Don't push me, you hippy prick,' said the drunk and knocked him down.

The other Special Branch man got to the counter as the clerk was pointing at the tramp and shouting, 'That one, that one.'

As the Special Branch man grabbed him the tramp swung a case off the counter and into his face with a violence that smashed his nose and cheekbone. He sank slowly, almost comically to the ground with a surprised look that faded as his eyes glazed into unconsciousness.

Ashby and Clifford, farther away than the other two, followed in quickly behind them and tried to close with the tramp. But the big drunk shouted, 'That makes four to one. Fuck that for a lark,' and aimed a sweeping backhander at Clifford, who stepped inside it, grabbed the man's lapels, pulled him forward and butted him in the face.

The drunk went down and Clifford stepped over him just as the tramp twisted out of Ashby's grip and raced across the station concourse towards the exit road that serves the boat-trains.

Ashby started after him, but Clifford shouted, 'Leave him! Leave him!'

He crouched down, drew the Remington, held it with both hands and sighted and squeezed the trigger in one fast flowing movement.

The tramp was about ten yards short of the exit road and just passing a free-standing DON'T FEED THE PIGEONS sign when he rose about two feet in the air and did an untidy forward roll, like an out-of-practice gymnast, ending up flat on his back staring up at the roof girders with eyes that saw nothing. The .221 Fireball had smashed the sixth and seventh cervical vertebrae and come out through his throat. He lay in a surprisingly large pool of blood which was still spreading as Clifford reached him.

'Jesus,' Clifford said in a voice that was hardly recognisable.

He had killed the wrong man.

She was slender, deep-bosomed and blacker than Kirote (blacker than the night), with a high-boned negro face and sloping head reminiscent in profile of Nefertiti. He called her Jenny. It was the nearest he could get to her first name, which sounded more like Yenny with a hiccup in the middle, the way a drunken German sailor might pronounce it.

She washed him, fed him, deloused him and nursed him back to health.

The rest of the inhabitants of shanty town assumed he was her ponce, which irritated those who felt she should have had a black ponce.

One of them was sufficiently irritated to try to stab him one night in a shebeen, when the liquor had been flowing. But as the man came at him, knife in hand, someone stuck out a foot and tripped him and someone else hit him on the head with an earthenware pot. Then they shoved him under the table and went on drinking.

From time to time someone poured beer over him to wake him up, but he didn't stir, and Abbott wondered if he was dead. Later, when he looked under the table, the man had gone.

Two kinds of drink were available, maize beer and a raw colourless spirit that burnt like lavatory disinfectant and had an aftertaste of creosote. Abbott stuck to the maize beer after spitting out the spirit. And the maize beer was strong enough. He didn't realise he was drunk till he tried to stand up. He remained seated and dignified, waiting for the strength to come back to his legs.

The shebeen was small and hot and badly lit by a smoky paraffin-lamp. The smell was indescribable and suddenly he couldn't take it any more. Outside the night was hot and black and full of stars.

'Christ, it's black,' he said, 'and so are you. I can hardly see you.'

He stood stock still till he was dark-adapted, but even then he could see only the crooked silhouettes of shanties in a faint haze of *starlight. And there were shadows everywhere. The cool night air made him feel drunk again and he grabbed Jenny's arm and held on to it.*

She was sweating and smelt warm and musky and he wondered what it would be like to have her. He also wondered whether the man who had tried to stab him was waiting in the shadows with a knife in his hand. It wasn't the first time a drunk had tried to stab him in shanty town, where drink usually led to violence or laughter.

The danger of being stabbed over a drink or a woman was endemic, but there was no danger of being betrayed to the police.

It was a comforting thought. Knives he could deal with.

16

WITHIN an hour of the shooting, Frank Smith had met Shepherd at Scotland Yard, given the Yard's Press Bureau a statement for the evening and Sunday papers, and reported the brief facts both to the Controller on his boat in the Solent (by a hook-up with the boat's radio-telephone) and to the Minister in his Belgravia flat. Both flapped.

'Christ Almighty,' the Controller said, 'can't I go away for five minutes without something going wrong?'

Smith calmed him down by pointing out that it would have gone wrong regardless of his presence and by reading him the statement he had prepared for the press. This said that the dead man was thought to be an IRA gunman who had gone to the left-luggage office to pick up weapons left there in a suitcase and had been shot in self-defence by Special Branch men trying to arrest him. It also said that for security reasons no further details would be issued at the moment.

The papers would buzz and speculate for a few days, then forget about it. And no doubt the IRA would deny the man was one of their members, but who would believe the IRA? He could easily, after all, have been a member of one of the Provisional splinter-groups.

The Controller grunted. Did Smith think he ought to come back and hold an inquiry? No, Smith thought he should stay where he was and enjoy the sailing. Smith was holding an inquiry himself and would report fully to the Controller on Monday.

Smith calmed the Minister down in a similar but vaguer and less specific way, saying in effect: Leave it to the professionals and don't worry. The Minister was not so much worried about the dead man and how he came to be dead as about the possible consequences to himself and his political career. After all he didn't *know* the dead man. He was just a dead man. Not even a constituent.

The Minister felt he was at a turning-point (he called it a watershed) in his career. The left wing of the party were dissatisfied with the Prime Minister and there was a plot to oust him. The Minister, who was favoured by the Left, was a possible successor. He was also favoured by the Prime Minister, of course, otherwise he wouldn't have been in the Cabinet. Sooner or later he would have to stop sitting on the fence, for which his large backside was eminently suited, and throw in his lot with one faction or the other. It was agonising trying to pick the winner. Meanwhile he wanted no scandal, no suggestion that he was falling down on his job, which included overall responsibility for security.

Smith assured him there would be no trouble and if there was it would be trivial and anyway the buck could always be passed. He didn't put it as bluntly as that but that was what he meant if you read between the lines. The Minister was very good at reading between the lines. In fact, he was so pleased and reassured he decided to visit his dying wife.

Finally, Smith started his inquiry.

'All right, how *did* Clifford make such a God Almighty cock-up?'

'He didn't,' said Shepherd, who always stood by his men.

'Shooting the wrong man isn't a cock-up?'

'He had no choice. It was a split-second decision. After all, if it *had* been Abbott, we'd be laughing.'

'But he was supposed to *know* if it was Abbott. He was supposed to recognise him. That was the whole idea of having him there, surely?'

Shepherd explained that Clifford had tackled the man from behind and didn't get a good look at him, that the man had a hat pulled down over his eyes and was dressed like a tramp – a disguise Abbott had used only a few days before.

'That's not enough to shoot a man for.'

'There was another thing – the way he reacted. Look, if you suddenly grab an ordinary member of the public he's scared, he's shaken, he freezes, he starts to protest. He doesn't react like this chap. React? He erupted. Like a bloody volcano.'

He shook his head. 'From Clifford's point of view it *had* to be Abbott.'

'Only it wasn't.' Smith sighed. 'I suppose it was one of those quarrelsome tramps that started the row outside the flats that night.'

'But why did he send someone else? I mean, what made him suspicious?'

'There was a bomb scare at the left-luggage office at Euston the other day.'

'So what?'

'He probably wondered whether the other left-luggage offices would get nervous and do some sort of check. A sweep with a metal-detector or something. It's the way his mind works. Or maybe he was just being extra cautious. . . . Over-protection, he calls it. A term used by chess-players, I believe.'

Shepherd thought for a while.

'Then Abbott would have had to be there – watching the whole thing.'

Smith nodded.

'Ready to scarper if things went wrong.'

'He couldn't have foreseen the shooting – merely the possibility that the man might get arrested and then released when the mistake was discovered.'

Smith and Shepherd were right. Abbott had been there, leaning against a Nestlé's vending machine at the top of the stairs that lead down to the Waterlooo Road.

And when he saw the gun in Clifford's hand he drew his own and took aim at him. But a girl helping an old woman across the concourse stepped into his line of fire. Then Clifford fired, and the running tramp went up in the air.

Abbott slipped the gun back in its holster, turned and started down the stairs. Then he saw that a man on the stairs was watching him open-mouthed.

'Going down to get a bus?' said Abbott.

'Er, yes,' said the man, trying to keep his voice steady, 'the, er, sixty-eight.'

His face had drained completely of colour.

'I'll walk down with you then,' said Abbott.

The man swallowed and nodded. They went down the stairs, turned right, then down the slope and out into the Waterloo Road. The man didn't say a word, didn't even look at him. Abbott saw that he was shaking.

'All you have to do,' Abbott said mildly, 'is get on the bus and go away.'

As they reached the stop a 68 pulled in.

'And here it is,' said Abbott. 'Aren't you lucky? You should back horses.'

The man stumbled in his haste to board the bus. Abbott watched it pull away. The man was sitting in his seat as if frozen to it.

'Fares, please,' the conductor said.

The man looked straight through him.

'Fares, please.' The conductor leant down and said it in his face.

'That man back there. He had a gun.' His eyes focused at last. 'He had a gun, I tell you. And staring eyes.'

'Look, chum, I'm busy,' the conductor said gently. 'Where d'you want to go, eh?'

'I don't know,' the man said, still confused by what seemed to him the experience of a lifetime. His mind, full of heroic fantasies, was not yet ready for mundane things. Later he would go to the police with an inaccurate and unclear story.

Abbott didn't know where to go either. He didn't want to go back to the flat; he wanted distraction. He wanted a blank programme put through his mind, like they do with a computer suffering from overstrain.

He took a cab to Earls Court. There was bound to be an exhibition on. Any exhibition would do. But he found the place shut, shuttered, bolted and barred, dead. It looked as if it had been dead for years.

He wandered into Old Brompton Road, then into Lillie Road and came to the West Centre Hotel, which is big, modern and from the outside slightly chilling. There he found the ideal distraction, the perfect blank programme: a chess congress.

Chess in England is usually played in conditions of near-squalor. Here the conditions were near-luxury. Three enormous rooms had been given over to the congress. In one was a grandmaster tournament, in another an open tournament. In the third were demonstration boards showing the progress of the grandmaster games with explanatory commentaries by chess masters or leading players. This was the room Abbott wandered into. He sat in an armchair and was soon lost in consideration of backward pawns, weak squares, the fearsomeness of the Dragon bishop and other intricacies of the game that Chandler called the greatest waste of human intelligence outside an advertising agency.

By an odd chance the Minister also wandered into the congress that afternoon. The sentimental impulse to visit his dying wife soon faded when he saw her. Within a few minutes he was trying to find excuses to leave the white-walled room with its hospital smell of death and flowers.

He knew the black girl had a five-o'clock matinée, but if he could get to her flat by about a quarter to four or even four there'd be time for. . . . Even half-past four. . . . She wasn't on till the second act; she didn't have to be there by five. . . . He suddenly realised his wife was talking to him.

'Stay with me,' she said, holding his hand. Her voice was weak, her hand clammy. 'Don't leave me.'

'Of course not,' he said, 'of course not. It's just that I've got to look in at this chess congress. You know, the one I opened in Fulham last week.'

'Don't go.'

'But I promised. And it *is* my constituency. I tell you what I'll do: I'll pop in there for half an hour and come straight back.'

'Please don't go.'

She had had a sudden premonition of death. It was in the room, she knew it was in the room. She could feel its presence though she couldn't see it. But she knew where it was. It was hovering behind the curtain. And when the curtain moved it wasn't the wind moving it, it was death. She would never see it of course, it would never show itself. It would wait behind the curtain till she fell asleeep, then come out and silently carry her off on the wings of darkness.

But if she kept awake, kept hold of her husband's hand, kept talking to him, death couldn't come out and take her away. As long as she remained awake death had to stay behind the curtain. She could feel herself getting sleepy but she clung to consciousness as she clung to her husband's hand.

'I won't be long, I promise you.'

'It can't come out if only you'll stay here.'

'What can't come out?'

'When the curtain moves it's getting impatient.'

Her mind was wandering again. He patted her hand.

'I'll be back presently,' he said, gently withdrawing his hand from hers.

Tears rolled down her face. She was very weak and wept easily and he attached no significance to it.

'Don't go,' she said. 'Please.'

The Minister drove quickly and got to the flat just before half-past four. He rang the bell, knocked on the door. No answer. He sighed. Well, he hadn't really expected her to be there. He didn't know what to do. He should have gone back to the hospital but couldn't face it. Having invented the excuse about the chess congress, he thought he might as well go there. He had no interest in the game and just about knew the moves, but it would be better than going back to the hospital.

He parked in the hotel's underground car-park, then went into the congress, where he was welcomed by the organisers, who took him round. He watched the grandmaster tournament for a few minutes then went into the demonstration room and listened to the expert commentaries without understanding a word.

'Very good,' he said to the organisers. 'Very impressive.'

Abbott was also in the room, but didn't see the Minister, and the Minister didn't see him. Not that they would have recognised each other anyway.

The Minister was then invited to the manager's office for a glass of champagne. On his way there he smiled benignly at a number of people he had never to his knowledge seen before and absently patted a dwarf on the head in mistake for a child.

In the manager's office he was jovial, talked fluently and knowingly about nothing in particular and drank two large glasses of a very dry and good champagne, which made him feel decidedly better. After a decent interval and a murmured protest he accepted a third glass.

He drove to the hospital feeling cheerful. With any luck his wife, who was heavily sedated, would be asleep and he'd be spared another session in that awful room. But his luck was out (or perhaps it was in). She wasn't asleep, she was dead.

It was a shock. He had been expecting it for weeks but it was still a shock. A bigger shock than he could have imagined. He felt weak and shaken. The doctor offered him a sedative but he refused (he knew enough not to mix sedatives with alcohol) and went home.

The flat seemed empty. Apart from himself and the daily help it had been empty ever since his wife went into hospital five weeks ago. But now that he knew she wasn't coming back the emptiness seemed to have a new dimension. And, strangely, the place seemed to echo. Which was impossible. It was thickly carpeted throughout, and the curtains were heavy and lined. Yet in his mind it seemed to echo.

Well, he was a free man now, after twenty years. He looked at his reflection in a wall-mirror.

'You're a free man now.'

But he didn't feel free, he felt alone. And in a curious way he missed her presence. But that was to be expected. If you had a dog for twenty years you'd miss it. And he was as fond of her as he could be of anyone other than himself. He even wished, in a vaguely sentimental moment, that he'd been a better husband.

At ten o'clock he was picking the black girl up from the theatre. He would have to be discreet, of course. If word got out. . . . People never understood these things.

Njala welcomed the head of the Russian trade delegation, Nikolai Nikolaievich Nezhmetdinov, with open arms and a bottle of vodka, and for half an hour refused to discuss anything but drink and women, two subjects he knew to be close to Nikolai Nikolaievich's heart. What he did not know was that Nikolai Nikolaievich considered them compensations for the sadness of an increasingly sad world, and at the same time part of that sadness. It was a very Russian thought and one that Njala, with all his astuteness, was unable to comprehend.

So Nikolai Nikolaievich smiled and listened and made appropriate noises and wondered when Njala would get down to business. Nikolai Nikolaievich, though nominally head of the trade delegation, knew very little about trade but a great deal about armaments. And Njala wanted arms that he could not get elsewhere, like the latest ground-to-air missiles and certain tactical nuclear weapons.

He was in the middle of a carefully engineered border dispute with one of his neighbours, whose country he aimed to take over. His long-term plan was to take over the countries of all his neighbours and form a Federated States of West Africa with himself at its head. This was part of a longer, even more ambitious plan in which he would come to dominate first central and eventually southern Africa, until in fact he ruled most of the continent. And if the Russians helped him unstintingly with armaments and technicians they would have not just a foothold but a permanent base in Africa such as even they had never envisaged in their grandest imperialist dreams.

And furthermore the Chinese would be reduced to a toehold in Tanzania and elsewhere. In other words, Russia would have a unified Black Africa indissolubly bound to her and this, with her control of the Middle East – the Mediterranean was already virtually a Russian lake – would make her the most powerful state in the world.

Nikolai Nikolaievich, who had heard most of this before, smiled one of his sad Russian smiles and pointed out that there were still problems in the way of controlling the Middle East, one of which was called Israel.

Israel. With a gesture of contempt Njala swept Israel aside as he imagined she would one day be swept into the sea by the combined forces of a united Africa and the United Arab Republic.

The trouble, as Nikolai Nikolaievich pointed out, was that the United Arab Republic was far from united and Black Africa even farther.

'True,' said Njala, 'but help me now and I'll make a beginning. And in two or three years, by a mixture of negotiation and force, I'll have a West African Federation.'

'Or you'll be a dead man.'

Njala shrugged. 'That is a chance many African leaders have to take. But what I need most of all, apart from the ability to stay alive, and for that I have considerable ability, is your help.'

'That you will get, in limited quantities – until you prove you can carry out your plans – and keep your promises. This last is very important.'

'Of course I will keep my promises. Otherwise you would thwart my plans. We depend on each other, don't you see that?'

'Oh yes, we see that. But do you?' He smiled sadly. 'Or do you imagine you can use us to the point where you are safely in power – in control, say, of some sort of African federation – and then drop us?'

'You underrate me. That would be cheap and foolish. My long-term interests lie with the Soviet Union. It is only certain Arab powers that think they can use the Soviet Union temporarily – take everything and give little or nothing in return.'

He paused, leaned forward and stared hard at Nikolai Nikolaievich.

'I, on the other hand, believe our interests are indissolubly linked. I believe you can help me to a position of pre-eminent power in Africa. I believe you can help me to maintain that power. I believe I cannot do without you. I also believe you cannot do without me – if you want to include Africa in your sphere of influence, that is.'

Nikolai Nikolaievich nodded. 'I've listened carefully to what you say, I like what you say, but I am not sure I altogether believe what you say.' He held up his hand. 'Please, I do not mean to be rude. People say something and at the time they mean it. Later, when circumstances change, they may mean something different.'

'Of course one cannot see what changes the future may bring. One can only work from present data. And present data point to a union of interests. Besides, I have everything to gain from alliance with you.'

'At the moment your alliance is with the British.'

'A temporary expedient. I am merely selling them oil while the bonanza lasts.'

'Not to mention uranium.'

'That, unfortunately, was part of the deal. However, our negotiations are for a three-year agreement. After that they will be digging their own oil out of the sea and are unlikely to want ours. In any case, they will not get it. Or our uranium.'

He smiled, showing his big white teeth.

'And then we are all yours.'

Nikolai Nikolaievich saw the force of the arguments but was doubtful. Russians are always doubtful, even of themselves. They suffer from a collective paranoia which help to make them exceptional chess players but can lead to overcaution and overreaction in international diplomacy.

However, they had reason to be cautious with Njala, who was as slippery as a greased pig. They had no doubt he would use them to gain power and then, while remaining friendly with them, gradually try to reduce their influence. Njala wanted no fetters on his ultimate power. It was a game the Russians had played and won before, though this time they had a formidable opponent and an expert player of games, especially dirty ones.

Nikolai Nikolaievich said he would report to the Politburo and if all went well a team of Russian military experts would visit Njala when he returned to Africa to discuss his needs and advise him.

After more vodka, vows of eternal friendship and brotherly love and trust, the Russian left and Njala and Arthur went down to the hotel lounge for tea – something they had only once done before. Half a dozen Special Branch men accompanied them and sat at nearby tables. Another two sat near the door.

Njala had with him a slim black executive briefcase of the type many businessmen carry.

Three olive-skinned young men – they could have been Spaniards or Cubans or Arabs or even Italians – came in smiling and talking. They looked like students. Each carried textbooks under his arm. One also carried a briefcase identical to Njala's. The Special Branch men at the door asked him to open it. It contained an envelope with some Arabic writing on it. Inside the envelope was a bracelet constructed of a circle of clasped hands, beautifully wrought in heavy gold.

'It's for my brother's twenty-first birthday,' the smiling young man explained.

The three young men went to sit at a table near Njala, but he recognised them and called them over to join him. They had tea and chatted and there was a good deal of laughter. After about half an hour they left.

When they got back to the penthouse Njala opened the briefcase and found he had taken the one containing the golden bracelet.

He handed the envelope to Arthur.

'You read Arabic. What does it say?'

'For our beloved brother and benefactor, who has made so much possible, and whom Allah preserve. May his shadow never grow shorter.'

'Well,' said Njala with his big white smile, 'it must be my lucky day.'

It was a beautiful trinket, and Njala loved trinkets. He put it on his right wrist and for the next few days constantly toyed with it and admired it.

17

AFTER watching the chess for about three hours and happily losing himself in analysing a king's pawn sacrifice by White in the Austrian attack against the Pirc, Abbott left the West Centre Hotel and took a taxi back to the flat.

Alice put her arms round him and hugged him. It wasn't just an automatic greeting, it was a necessity for contact. The touch of him, the feel of his body against hers, a living warmth that was as reassuring and comforting as the warmth of the sun.

'You've been so long I was beginning to worry.' She looked at him closely. 'Are you all right?'

'I'm fine.'

'There's nothing wrong?'

'No. Everything's for the best in the best of all possible worlds.'

The edge of bitterness in his voice made her want to question him further but she decided not to. There was something about his manner that discouraged questions.

'I was about to start dinner.'

'Let's eat out.'

'Where?'

'Where you like.'

'I know – where we used to. That Italian place in Kensington Church Street. Remember? And let's have a table upstairs, in the corner by the window. Like we did that night . . . that last time we went there.'

He nodded absently. 'Sure.'

'I'll book a table. What time? Nine?'

'Ten.'

'That's a bit late, isn't it?'

He didn't answer.

She hesitated. 'You *are* all right?'

'I'm fine. Got anything to drink?'

'Only some plonk.'

'That'll do.'

For the next hour she chatted away and asked him if he liked her new dress and he said yes and sat and stared out of the window and drank the red wine.

Just before nine he ordered a cab.

'But it's only a few minutes to the restaurant.'

'We're not going to the restaurant. Not yet.'

They took the cab and drove round Hyde Park in the gathering darkness. Abbott told the driver to wait near Marble Arch and left Alice in the cab. He walked down Park Lane till he came opposite Njala's hotel. He found a place where he could watch the front entrance and waited.

After a time a black Daimler, accompanied by two police cars and an escort of motor-cycle outriders, drew up outside the entrance. Njala and Arthur, surrounded by Special Branch men, including Shepherd and Clifford, came out and got into the Daimler.

Njala was smiling and laughing and talking, obviously in good spirits. Abbott got little more than a glimpse of him. A reasonable shot at him, even if he'd had the rifle, would have been out of the question : he would have almost certainly killed or injured other people.

Uniformed police held up the traffic, and the black Daimler and its escort pulled away.

'Goodbye,' said Abbott softly. 'And gather plenty of rose-buds.'

Then he walked back to the cab, which drove them to the restaurant in Kensington Church Street. Alice held his hand all the way.

They shook hands with Vittorio and sat upstairs at the round table by the window. Abbott was still a little absent-minded, but after he had ordered a bottle of Chianti and had a couple of glasses he began to relax a little and look at Alice.

She was not beautiful but in some indefinable way she felt

beautiful, or almost beautiful, perhaps because she knew Abbott was looking at her and liked what he was looking at. Her long hair shone where it caught the light, which was discreet and shaded, and the new dress really did suit her, setting off the flow of neck and shoulder and breast. Even her squint did not detract from the softness and clearness of her eyes, when she raised them. Or so it seemed to Abbott. He wondered why he had ever thought her plain. Of course the light helped and so did the wine.

A lot of men like women for sex or amusement or convenience, but don't really like them as women. Abbott did, for all the trouble they cause. Perhaps it was this fundamental sympathy for women that was picked up by that infallible radar they all possess.

Throughout the meal Alice touched him in small ways whenever she could, touched his hand when passing the salt or making little gestures, touched his arm when she smiled or wanted to draw his attention to something, touched his shoulder when she removed what she imagined was a piece of loose cotton from his jacket. And finally, when the meal was finished, just reached across the table and took his hand.

He felt even more relaxed. At first he thought it was the wine, and at first it was the wine. But then it was her, her presence, her gestures, the way she moved her hands, the way she smoothed her hair back tightening the dress across her breasts, her earnestness, her shyness because of the squint, and above all her femininity which seemed, gently and unobtrusively, to pervade everything and print the very air with its presence.

By this time Njala and Arthur, closely attended by Shepherd and the trigger-happy Clifford, had made an uneventful flight from London Heliport to Leyfield Hall.

Njala hated flying, especially by night. Above all, he hated helicopters, which were noisy and flimsy and, he was sure, unsafe. He hated flying through the black womb of night and death, which was how he pictured it, and he slipped his hand inside his shirt and fingered his voodoo beads and sweated. He laughed and joked to cover his fears, but Arthur knew about them and smiled to himself. He liked Njala to suffer, it so rarely happened.

They landed on the back lawn at Leyfield Hall in the brilliant light of arc lamps and a ring of armed men with dogs.

Leyfield Hall, gloomy and mid-Victorian though it was from the outside, was extremely comfortable and what estate agents call well appointed inside and, to Njala's surprise, centrally heated and draught-free.

'Amazing,' he said to Arthur. 'Amazing. The English used to be quite primitive in these things. It must be all those package holidays. The cultural interchange. Fish and chips in Venice, double windows in Petersfield. No wonder they conquered three-quarters of the world. The sun never sets on fish and chips. Remarkable. You do follow me, Arthur?'

'Perfectly, Your Excellency.'

Njala's suite on the first floor pleased him even more.

There was an enormous sitting-room with a large picture window to the west, overlooking a side lawn and the summer-house. On the south side, which was the front of the house, were two tall windows overlooking a vast lawn bounded by a stream beyond which was a mixed wood of deciduous trees. Off-centre of the lawn was an old tall spreading cedar with that air of age and elegant melancholy peculiar to cedars.

Immediately in front of the house was a gravel drive and forecourt bordered partly by a line of massed and brilliant hydrangeas, partly by a line of gloomy-looking rhododendrons thick enough to conceal a man.

The room itself was covered with an off-white fitted carpet overlaid with two long Persian rugs like runners. The rest of the room contained comfortable antique furniture, including a Queen Anne sofa, a couple of Queen Anne wing-chairs with cabriole legs, an eighteenth-century mahogany break-front bookcase and, by the west window, a magnificent flat-topped mahogany writing-desk of the Chippendale period, which particularly pleased Njala.

'I like that,' he said to Arthur. 'I can work there.'

In fact he liked the whole room, even the pictures on the wall, which included a Cotman water-colour, though pictures meant little to Njala apart from decoration.

Leading off the sitting-room were a large bedroom with a four-poster bed, and a small intimate dining-room in case Njala wanted to dine alone or with a woman. Off the bedroom was a dressing-room, off which were a bathroom and lavatory.

The whole suite was self-contained and the only entrance was from the corridor through the heavy oak double doors of the sitting-room. Outside the doors an armed Special Branch man was aways on duty.

Along the rest of the corridor were rooms for those guests who were not sleeping with Njala, a room for Arthur and one for Shepherd, who regarded himself as the last line of defence.

Njala sat at the Chippendale desk in the sitting-room and sipped a glass of pale sherry while Arthur unpacked the books they had brought and arranged them in the break-front bookcase.

'You know, Arthur, I think it's time we did a little homework on our assassin. What was his name?'

'His real name?' Arthur shrugged. 'The name on his passport was Wilson.'

'Tell the embassy to dig up everything they've got on him. Tell them to cable the Minister of the Interior for the file on him, then put through a call to the Chief of Police – I'll speak to him myself. He'll know more than any file, he did most of the interrogating.'

'Yes, Your Excellency.'

Arthur crossed to the door.

'Oh, and Arthur, I know their policemen are wonderful but. . . .'

He made a little gesture.

'Sir?'

'You didn't forget to pack my gun?'

Frank Smith and Joan Abbott had dinner in Smith's flat. She cooked *blanquette de veau* with wild rice and mushrooms and a sauce of her own making. He opened a bottle of Veuve Cliquot.

'Why champagne?'

'We're celebrating.'

'Celebrating what?'

'I'm not absolutely sure. Just celebrating.'

She smiled. 'I like that.'

During the meal they spoke little. He was still preoccupied with the events of the afternoon. She was feeling nervous, and in some way out of place, as if she were taking advantage of him.

'That was a lovely meal. You really are a very good cook.'

'I like cooking.'

He took a sip of champagne, studied her covertly because he thought staring was rude.

'Joan, is something wrong?'

'No. No, of course not. You've been . . . very kind.'

'I mean, you're not, er . . . unhappy here or anything?'

'Good heavens, no. On the contrary, you've been . . . most kind.'

'So you keeping saying. But you don't seem . . . well, very relaxed.'

She was silent and fiddled with her glass.

'I feel I'm . . . imposing on you.'

'Imposing? I like having you here. Besides, you can't go back to the flat, some of Shepherd's men are still there – on the off-chance that Richard might show up some time.'

'I could . . . go to my cousin's. I'm sure she wouldn't mind.'

'Aren't you happy here?'

'Very.'

'Then . . . ?'

'Look, you – you took pity on me, you took me in, looked after me. And what did I do? Climbed straight into bed with you.'

'Yes, shocking, wasn't it? Still, I closed my eyes and thought of England.'

'Frank, please, this is serious. I felt I might've . . . compromised you in some way. Or led you into thinking you might've compromised me.'

'Oh, you did. You certainly compromised me. And I compromised you. In fact, it could be said we compromised each other. And I suggest we go on compromising each other. For a long time to come. I find it a most satisfying experience, in every sense of the word. Besides. . . .'

He paused and cleared his throat to gather confidence.

'Besides . . . I like you.'

She smiled at him. 'It would be rather awful if you didn't.'

'By God, for a shy man I'm getting bold, aren't I? Perhaps it's the champagne. Shall we have some more?'

When Alice and Abbott got to bed that night Abbott was drunk, though it would have been difficult to tell. His speech was coherent if a little too deliberate. So were his movements. There was a lack of fluidity in them.

They lay side by side naked in the darkness of the moon-splashed room, arms round each other.

'I don't think I can make love tonight. It's the drink.'

'You think that's all that matters? Lying here beside you is enough, just feeling you against me.'

She smiled in the darkness. Yes, and waking in the night knowing he was there, feeling him there, feeling some little movement as he turned in his sleep. It was enough, and more. If only he would stay there. If only. . . . Now don't get sad, she told herself.

'Best of all,' she said, 'I like waking up in the morning. And before I'm properly awake knowing I'm happy but not knowing why. Then all of a sudden knowing why. Because you're there. Does that sound silly?'

He was drifting off into sleep, half-hearing her words, his mind full of hazy unconnected images as in a waking dream. Just before he dropped off he saw the running tramp go up in the air and over into an untidy roll, ending up on his back, arms outstretched like a man crucified.

At night the fruit-sellers put up their stalls at the street-corners and lit them with candles. From Jenny's verandah he could see the lights coming on one after another, worrying the darkness like fireflies.

One night he walked up there with Jenny on his arm, through the silent almost deserted commercial quarter, into the shopping-centre noisy with argument and laughter, alive with people and flickering candlelight, most of the men wearing T-shirts with Njala's picture on them, most of the women in cheap cotton dresses only dignified by the slow poetry of their haunch-rolling walk.

They crossed Njala Square with its modern hotels and sidewalk cafés where tourists, sailors and fashionable whores strolled and hunted in the evening promenade.

He had grown a beard and Jenny had got him some seaman's clothes so that he would pass unnoticed. She even got him a peaked seaman's cap, which reminded him of a mysterious character in a German novel who wore a similar sort of cap (der Mann in der Kapitänsmütze) and who kept popping up at awkward times like the incarnation of a bad conscience.

'That's me,' he said. 'I'm their bad conscience.'

'You're what?'

'The man in the Kapitänsmütze,' he said.

They left the square and the strollers and the flickering lights below and climbed a short steep hill to Njala Park. He found the tree and climbed it. The gun was still there in its case, wrapped in oilskin.

When they got back to the bungalow he took it out of the case, cleaned the grease off, examined it and assembled it. It was in perfect working order.

'What do you want another gun for?' she said.

'I don't know,' he said. 'It might come in handy. Look at it, it's a beautiful job, isn't it?'

'Beautiful,' she said. 'And obscene.'

18

NJALA spent a womanless night and worked till past three in the morning with Arthur and a financial adviser on the oil and uranium production figures and prices and what political concessions might be gained if prices were lowered and if the concessions would be worth it.

Soon after three came a cable, relayed through the embassy, that his cousin Joseph Omatu was planning a coup. He immediately cabled orders to the Chief of Police and an army general he more or less trusted to arrest Omatu and his family and execute them on the spot. Any known supporters of Omatu were to be similarly executed and a division of picked troops sent to that part of the country inhabited by Omatu's tribe. Any incipient rebellion or disorder there was to be speedily and bloodily crushed.

Njala then discussed other aspects of the oil and uranium negotiations for an hour, then went to bed because he could see the other two were sleepy and no longer thinking straight. He was tired himself, tired but wakeful and slightly irritated for lack of a woman. For two pins he'd take that damned helicopter and fly it back to London. . . . But that would hardly be sensible. And this time he had to be sensible.

The Controller's thoughts were also on London. He felt he really couldn't stay down there sailing happily on the Solent while God knows what was going on up in London. Besides, it was supposed to be typical of the British Establishment to be mindlessly weekending in the country while international crises broke out all over. So, late that Saturday, he reluctantly left the waterside pub, the beer, the jokes and all that nautical chat beloved of amateur sailors and drove his 1967 Bristol back to London.

Soon after midnight he rang Frank Smith, who was in bed.

'Don't move,' said Joan. 'Let it ring.'

'I've no intention of moving,' said Smith. 'Or of letting it ring.'

He lifted the receiver. 'Smith.'

'Ah, Frank. Controller here. I'm a bit worried, I'd like a word.'

'Sorry,' said Smith, 'I'm busy.'

'Busy?'

'Busy in bed.'

'I beg your pardon?' said the Controller. Then the penny began to drop. 'Oh. . . . Oh, I see. . . .'

'What about tomorrow? At the office. Say ten o'clock.'

'Er, fine,' said the Controller, confused. 'Fine. Er, Frank, I'm awfully sorry to have, er . . . disturbed you.'

'Not at all. It's a sensation I've never experienced before and it's quite pleasant. Goodnight, sir.'

The Controller spent a restless and uncomfortable night.

The Minister picked up the black girl after the theatre, didn't mention his wife's death, and drove her to the flat in Fulham, where they sat in comfortable armchairs on opposite sides of a low round glass coffee-table – she naked, he fully dressed – and drank champagne, as was their custom. It made him feel daring and a little depraved (he had a print of *Déjeuner sur l'herbe* in his flat).

Later, in bed, while they were making love, he told her about his wife's death.

'Don't you feel anything about it?'

'Oh yes. Quite a lot. I was very fond of her.'

'And you can still do this? Tonight?'

'Of course.'

'Boy, you're cool.'

'What difference does it make whether I do it tonight o tomorrow night or next year?'

'Yeah, but don't you feel it's a bit . . . well, disrespectful?'

'Not nearly as disrespectful as when she was alive.'

Sunday morning broke clear and sunny and suspiciously warm for early May. We'll pay for this later, the wiseacres said – and no doubt they were right because if you wait long enough you're bound to be right about the English weather.

Frank Smith met the Controller in his office at ten, and the Controller was worried.

'I don't like it.'

'What in particular?'

'Nothing in particular. Everything. The whole set-up.'

'But we're all right so far. I mean, Abbott doesn't even know where the house is.'

Smith said this with hope rather than conviction.

'And how long is it going to take him to find out? I mean, it's not like trying to hide some tuppenny-ha'penny defector. It's a head of state we're trying to hide. And he's not exactly a shrinking violet.'

'The key to the whole operation is to get those negotiations over as quickly as possible – and get him out of the country.'

'You've made arrangements?'

'There's an aircraft on stand-by at Gatwick ready to take off at a moment's notice.'

'So all we have to do is hurry the bastard up.'

'Yes, sir, that is all.'

'Frank,' said the Controller, 'I can do without irony at this time in the morning.'

'I'll go down and see him now, shall I? Perhaps I can . . push him along a bit.'

'It can't hurt, I suppose. What about the Minister? D'you think you should take him along?'

'His wife died last night.'

'Yes, I heard it on the radio. You think it will affect him?'

Smith thought. 'No. And his presence might add weight. Anyway, it'll *look* more important if I have a Minister of the Crown with me. Providing he doesn't keep falling asleep, that is.'

The Controller nodded, doodled on his blotter, tapped his teeth with a fingernail. .

'That balls-up at Waterloo. Why *didn't* Shepherd have a couple of dozen men there?'

'Because they'd have looked like coppers and Abbot would've spotted them. Besides, they'd've got in each other's way when the balloon went up. Anyway, that was Shepherd's point. And for once I think he was right.'

'But his method didn't work very well either, did it?'

'That was because of the two drunks. Put it down to bad luck, coincidence, fate, providence, whatever you like, but in my experience it buggers up more plans than any amount of human stupidity.'

The Controller nodded his agreement, tapped his yellowing teeth again.

'Where the hell *is* Abbott? He hasn't got any money as far as we know. We're watching all his friends. Where *is* he?'

'With a woman.'

'A *woman?*'

'That's what Joan thinks.'

'On what evidence?'

'No evidence. Instinct, intuition, female radar, or maybe she read it in the tea-leaves. Actually, he spoke to her on the phone and she said she could hear it in his voice.'

'Hear what?'

'That he'd got a woman.'

'She could *hear* it in his voice?'

'That's what she said.'

'Christ.'

'She probably knows him better than anyone.'

'Yes, I know, but. . . .'

The Controller stopped, spread his hands, not knowing what to say.

'Have you any better suggestions?'

'No, but. . . .' Again he stopped.

'He gets on well with women. I'm not suggesting he's the office Casanova or anything like that, but the women seem to like him. So he could be shacking up with some girl somewhere, I suppose.'

'Do we know any of his girl-friends?'

'No, but Alice might. She was his secretary before he went to Africa. She might remember if women rang him up or left messages for him. That sort of thing.'

'Good point. Get her in.'

'She's on a week's leave. But I could try her home.'

He reached for the phone.

In Hyde Park, far enough from Speakers' Corner not to be disturbed by the speeches and the heckling, Abbott was sitting on a bench in the pleasantly warm morning sun talking to a man called Jaka ben Yehuda, who spoke fluent English. 'The subsequent problems, providing you have somewhere to lie low for a few weeks, are simple.'

'I have somewhere to go to for two or three months if necessary – anyway, till the hubbub dies down.'

'Then the rest is easy. We will issue you a genuine passport in a false name and fly you out. It may be necessary to adopt a simple disguise like growing a beard and dyeing your hair. But I see no problems.'

'I also want to take a girl with me.'

'Is she connected with you? I mean, is there a known connection with you?'

'No. She was once my secretary for a few months a couple of years ago. That's all.'

'Then that is even simpler. She travels as a tourist on the same plane or a later plane.'

'Thank you. I cannot tell you what this means to me.'

'No more, I imagine, than the life of an Israeli agent meant to us.'

Jaka ben Yehuda stood up to go.

'One thing. I know you've visited our country several times. But living there could be another matter. You might not like it. And there is always the danger of war. It is not the safest place in the world.'

'Apart from my own country there is no place I would sooner live. Or, if necessary, die.'

Abbott wanted to reiterate his thanks but did not know what to say. Words seemed inadequate.

Perhaps Jaka ben Yehuda sensed something of this. A brief smile lit the pallor of his face, a pallor acquired by eleven years in a Russian concentration camp and which no amount of sun would darken.

'You are our friend,' he said. 'We remember that.' And shook hands and walked away under the trees.

Yes, they remembered their friends all right, even longer than they remembered their enemies.

Abbott went back to the flat and found it empty.

The Controller apologised for bringing Alice in when she was supposed to be on leave, especially on a Sunday morning (though Alice couldn't see anything special about that). However, it *was* important and it had to do with Richard Abbott.

Alice kept her head lowered, as she always did, but felt what seemed like a cold stone in her stomach.

'The problem is: where is he? Where *can* he be? You see, we know he has very little money, which rules out hotels or boarding-houses, and we've checked on friends and relatives. So what are we left with?'

Alice looked at the floor and waited.

'For reasons we won't bother you with,' said Frank Smith, 'we think he might be living with a woman.'

Alice kept her head lowered and nodded gravely. 'Yes, that's possible, I suppose.'

'Now you were his secretary for some time before we went to Africa,' said the Controller. 'And when he was living apart from his wife.'

'Now, do you remember if he had any girl-friends during that time?' said Smith.

'Oh yes, two or three. Let's see, there was one called Barbara, one called Janice, I think, or was it Janet? Anyway, something like that. And then there was a third whose name sounded something like Poldi.'

'Short for Leopoldina,' said Smith. 'Was she Austrian?'

'She had a sort of German-sounding accent.'

'Did you ever meet any of them?' said the Controller.

'No. Only spoke to them on the phone.'

'D'you know if he slept with any of them?' said Smith.

The Controller coughed in embarrassment. He thought Smith might have used a more delicate word like intimate.

Alice kept her head lowered and said : 'Men usually sleep with their girl-friends, don't they?'

'D'you know where any of them live?'

'No. But I may have their phone numbers in my old note-books.'

'See if you can find them, will you?'

'And did you?'

'Quite easily.'

'And were they pleased?'

'The Controller said : Smart girl. We could do with a few more like you.'

Abbott smiled.

'But at least they've worked out you're living with a woman.'

. 'So are about twenty million other men in the country. It would be a rather lengthy process of elimination. Anyway, what do you want to do this afternoon?'

'Well, there's a film on at the Curzon I'd quite like to see. . . .' She shook her head. 'No. I think it's daft to go out. Why take risks when you don't have to?'

'It's a lovely day, though. Might be the best for a long time. Who knows? So what about a drive in the country in whatsername?'

'Florence.'

'And have a picnic and lie in the sun and do whatever lovers do.'

'Oh, smashing. What a smashing idea. . . . No. No, we can't. The risk.'

He put his hands round her solemn young face and kissed her eyes, her ears, her forehead and her mouth with a delicacy that took her breath away.

'Time,' he said between kisses, 'is all we've got. And not very much of it.'

'But—'

'No buts.'

'If you don't let me go I won't be able to think straight. No, don't let me go. Whatever you do, don't let me go.'

He let her go. She sighed and shook herself as if coming out of a dream.

'What shall we take?'

'A bottle of plonk.'

'To *eat*.'

'I don't know. Sandwiches. Whatever you like.'

'I've got some pâté, cervelat, dolce latte— What are you smiling at?'

'Several things, including you.'

'You think I'm funny?'

'Yes. And very attractive.'

19

SMITH and the Minister drove down to Petersfield in time for lunch and found Njala in high spirits, mainly because he was looking forward to a good day and an even better night.

Meanwhile, what could he do for the gentlemen?

'Well, as you know,' said the Minister, 'the President of the Board of Trade and two of his advisers will be down after lunch to continue negotiations—'

'Yes, amazing, isn't it? The civil service working on a Sunday. It's a wonder the stars don't start from their spheres.'

'Now while we don't want to hurry you in any way—'

'You won't, Minister, you won't.'

Njala gave him a big white smile.

'We would appreciate it if negotiations could be concluded as expeditiously as possible.'

'In view of the dangers of the situation,' put in Smith.

'You know,' said Njala with another of those big white smiles, 'I really am beginning to think this whole production's a British plot to get those concessions on the cheap.'

'Your Excellency,' the Minister began, 'I assure you—'

'My dear Minister, I wouldn't put anything past the British, especially when it comes to business. Look at Biafra. If there'd been anything like social justice in this world – which there isn't – the British Government, which is always talking about social justice, would have gone to the aid of poor little Biafra. But they didn't. It would have cost too much.'

'Your Excellency, I really must protest—'

'Or take South Africa. Now anti-apartheid's fine and doesn't cost a thing. But try interfering with trade – South Africa's your third biggest customer, I believe – and you'll have trouble.

Smith cut in hard. 'Sir, neither money nor politics is my line.

Security is. And the security situation, as we've tried to impress on you, is extremely dangerous. And the longer you stay here the more dangerous it gets – literally by the hour.'

Njala treated him to one of those big white smiles.

'My dear Mr Smith, I'm used to danger. I've lived with it all my life. You wouldn't believe the number of people who've tried to assassinate me. Or perhaps you would. Anyway, I feel safer here than I've felt anywhere outside my own fortified palace – what with all those armed men out there and whatsis-name, the sharpshooter in the summer-house.'

'Sergeant Clifford.'

'A quite extraordinary marksman, I'm told. With lightning reactions.'

He strolled to the west window and glanced down at the summer-house, where Clifford was sitting motionless at an open window. Across his knees was the Armalite-based sniper's rifle that had been specially made for Njala's assassination and was now ironically for his protection.

'There's His Nibs,' said Clifford, 'having a butcher's.'

Shepherd, who was also in the summer-house, said, 'Good view?'

'Good enough.'

'What do you think of the rest of the arrangements?'

'Pretty fair, Guv. Got all the weak points covered. And if he comes round this side of the house he's a dead man, isn't he?'

All the while Clifford idly, perhaps unconsciously caressed the rifle rather as a man even just after love-making might idly run his hand over the woman's body because its curves and hollows and softness and dampness and the feel of female skin still gave him a sensual and loving pleasure.

During lunch Njala had the radio playing constantly though softly in the background. It was tuned to LBC for the newscasts.

'I do apologise for the radio,' Njala said, 'but I happen to be fascinated by news, particularly at the moment because if there's another attempted coup I should like to be, if not the first, at least one of the first to know.'

189

Abbott drove the ancient and slightly ailing Florence (she could have done with a rebore and a new set of points and plugs) to a place near Box Hill that was usually deserted even on a warm Sunday afternoon.

'How do you like her?' said Alice happily.

'Sorry?'

'Florence.'

'Oh, Florence. Fine, fine. Very nice.'

In fact, he found her noisy and cramped and the ride choppy as it always is with short-wheelbase cars.

'It's nice with the roof open, isn't it? Helps to keep it cool on warm days.'

It also helped to get rid of the fumes that were coming up through the floor from a leaky exhaust.

By about two o'clock they found an isolated spot away from the road and parked Florence in the shade of some elder trees.

'Isn't it marvellous? And peaceful? You'd think you were out in the wilds, wouldn't you? Miles from anywhere.'

Her face was flushed with happiness.

They ate their picnic lunch of hard-boiled eggs and chives, with brown bread and butter, pâté, cervelat and dolce latte, and drank a litre of red wine.

Then they took a short walk, hand in hand, through some woods.

'The smell of meadowsweet in damp woods,' he said.

'What?'

'It's something I shall always remember.'

'What does it smell like?'

'It's very fragrant and has small creamy flowers.'

'I can't smell it. Or even see it.'

He pointed. 'That's it, there. But it's too early for the flowers. Or the fragrance. That comes in June.'

'Why do you always remember it?'

'Something to do with childhood, I expect. Everything's more vivid then.'

They walked on for a bit and the sun strengthened surprisingly and they began to feel sleepy and lay down in the shade of some trees and put their arms round each other and kissed a little and cuddled a little, as if seeking comfort or reassurance rather than passion, the comfort and reassurance of each other's presence. Presently they fell asleep or rather half-asleep, dozing, dreaming, waking and touching each other, dozing again and gradually getting closer to each other.

Soon after four o'clock they woke up, smiled at each other, kissed each other and strolled back to the car, holding each other. They had a coffee from a thermos flask and stared at the greenness of the country and the wind rippling the grass, and thought of nothing in particular, just taking pleasure in the peace and the countryside and being together.

They leant against the car, the sun warming their bodies, staring at the greenness without really seeing it, communicating physically and mentally without touching or speaking. It was an idyllic moment, the end of an idyllic afternoon.

In London something terrible was happening, but they only learned about it later.

The negotiations at Leyfield Hall were going well – well for Njala, that is, the President of the Board of Trade and his negotiators having had instructions that speed was more important than profit.

Njala was sharp and attentive as usual but still kept half an ear on the radio.

Soon after four came the announcement that a bomb had been thrown into a meeting of Jewish ex-servicemen in Trafalgar Square, killing six and wounding a number of others. The newsreader wasn't sure of the exact number of casualties since reports were still coming in.

The bomb, in a slim black executive briefcase, had been thrown into the crowd from a speeding car that had shot out of the Strand, crossed the square and disappeared into Pall Mall. The car was found abandoned in St James's Square, where the occupants, two men, had apparently transferred to another car and disappeared.

Njala switched the radio off and said, 'As you know I am

an anti-Zionist, but I abhor terrorism and indiscriminate killing. I suggest we stand in silence for one minute and suspend further negotiations till tomorrow.'

Which they did, everyone looking grave and solemn, especially Njala, who occasionally fingered his heavy gold bracelet.

Abbott drove Alice to a little country pub near Ockley where they serve simple and good meals and they had steak-and-kidney pie and a bottle of burgundy.

'What do you want to do this evening?'

'Be all suburban and go home and sit on the sofa and watch some of those lousy programmes on the box. And get sleepy. And go to bed with my beautiful man. Did you know you were beautiful?'

'I bet you say that to all the fellas.'

On the way home they switched on the car radio and caught the news about the bomb. Black September had claimed responsibility for it.

They drove the rest of the way in silence. Alice began to feel cold and slipped on a cardigan.

The remaining fragments of the briefcase and bomb were carefully assembled on the Controller's desk.

With the Controller were Smith, two experts from the Yard's bomb squad, Shepherd and the Minister.

'It's a new type of bomb,' said one of the experts, 'or rather a modification and improvement of the old type. They have managed to contain the exploding fragments within an expanding circle about two to four feet above ground. Which makes it, or course, an extremely effective anti-personnel weapon.'

He went on to explain a great deal more about the bomb's structure, mechanism, detonation device and fragmentation qualities which the other expert understood perfectly. Nobody else did.

The Controller thanked them warmly and the two experts left.

'What I'd like to know,' said the Controller, 'is how they got that dam' briefcase-bomb into the country. With all the sophisticated gubbins we've got at the airport I'd have thought we'd have smelt it out in no time.'

'Perhaps the IRA gave them a hand,' said Smith.

'I'd have thought the IRA would have enough trouble smuggling their own stuff in, without helping outsiders.'

'Anyway,' said the Minister, 'there's no known connection between the IRA and Black September, is there?'

'The fact that a connection isn't known,' said the Controller, 'doesn't disprove its existence.'

There was a silence. Then Shepherd spoke.

'There's a connection between Njala and Black September.'

'We know all about that,' said the Controller. 'He had a secret meeting with them in Beirut – at least, he thought it was secret – when he was supposed to be there on holiday.'

'He could've brought the briefcase over for them. Nobody checks the luggage of a visiting head of state.'

'Oh come now,' said the Minister, 'surely you're not suggesting President Njala would—'

'That's exactly what I am suggesting,' said Shepherd.

'On what grounds?'

Shepherd sighed. 'Well, not much, I'm afraid. Just a couple of odd things that don't mean anything by themselves, but taken together and with a bit of hindsight might add up to something.'

'Your exposition fascinates me,' the Minister said dryly. 'Do go on.'

'I'd sooner let Sergeant Roberts tell you, if you don't mind. He was on duty at the hotel yesterday and he's a bright lad – real bright. I've got him outside.'

Sergeant Roberts was brought in and Shepherd said, 'You know some of these gentlemen and the others you don't need to know. Tell 'em what you told me.'

Roberts was young and intelligent-looking. He cleared his throat and was nervous at first but soon gained confidence.

'Well,' he said, 'President Njala and his secretary came down into the lounge for tea yesterday afternoon. Well, that was a bit unusual for a start. I've only seen 'em do that once before, when there was a fashion show there and it was pretty obvious they had come to clock the birds. I mean to—'

'It's all right, Sergeant,' said the Controller, 'we know what you mean. Go on.'

'Well, he's not often in the hotel in the afternoon, but when he is he has tea up in his suite.'

'Still,' said Shepherd. 'If he fancied a cup of char in the lounge for a change, what's wrong with that?'

'Nothing, sir. That's just what I said to myself. The other thing was he was carrying one of those cheap black executive briefcases. You know the type : a dime a dozen, as they say.'

The Controller pointed to the fragments of the one on his desk.

'Like that one? Or what's left of it?'

'It's not easy to say but . . . I'd think so. The other funny thing was : why was he carrying it himself? I mean, why wasn't the secretary carrying it for him? Of course, I didn't think anything of it – I mean they were just – well, the sort of silly idle thoughts that drift through your mind when you've got nothing better to do.'

'I think your thoughts were neither silly nor idle,' said the Controller. 'I think they show the kind of instinctive perception that may take you quite a long way in your job.'

'Then these young students come in – well, that's what I supposed they were. They were casually dressed and all that and carrying books. And one of them had a briefcase – just like the one President Njala had with him. Well, I had a look at the books. You know, it's easy enough to cut lumps out of the pages and hide a gun in a book.'

He paused.

'Then I had a look at the briefcase. All it contained was an envelope with what looked like Arabic writing on the outside. Inside it was a real big heavy gold bracelet, made entirely of clasped hands. Must've cost a bomb. Anyway, the young man – nice-looking young chap he was – smiled and said it was for his brother's birthday. Anyway, he had a receipt with him for it – from some jeweller's in Paris. Then he and the others went

194

towards a table, but Njala obviously recognised them and called them over and they all sat down and had tea with him and laughed and joked. And then they left. With their books and their briefcase.'

Roberts paused again, a note of bitterness coming into his voice. 'Of course, if I'd've been a bit brighter I might have asked for another look at that briefcase.'

'Sergeant Roberts,' said the Controller, 'there was no earthly reason why you should ask to examine that briefcase again. And your brightness is not in question. Quite the reverse. It will in fact be remembered. And not just by me, will it, Superintendent Shepherd?'

'Indeed not, sir,' said Shepherd.

'Thank you, Sergeant Roberts,' said the Controller. 'And I mean thank you.'

Roberts gave a brief nod and left.

Shepherd said, 'I've only one thing to add. When Njala arrived on Saturday night, I noticed he was wearing a heavy gold bracelet of clasped hands. I noticed it because he kept looking at it and fiddling with it.'

'So,' said the Controller, 'it looks as if our friend and ally whom we are going to so much trouble to protect could have helped Black September to kill half a dozen people in Trafalgar Square.'

'Now wait a minute,' said the Minister, 'there must be other bracelets like that in the world.'

'And thousands of briefcases,' said Smith.

'Admittedly it looks suspicious,' said the Minister, 'but it could – it just could have been a coincidence.'

'I agree,' said the Controller, 'and by a coincidence of fate and genetics I could've been Shirley Temple.'

'Anyway, we've no proof. Absolutely no proof.'

'Just as well, isn't it?' said Smith. 'Or we *would* be in a fucking awkward situation.'

'It just doesn't bear thinking about,' said the Minister.

'You know,' said Smith, 'I'm beginning to think it wasn't such a bad idea we had a couple of years back of knocking Njala off.'

'Smith,' said the Controller, using his surname for the first time in years, 'that will do. Especially in front of a Minister of the Crown.'

The Minister looked at them with what he hoped was concealed dislike. The bastards were sending him up in their polite snide civil service way.

Alice and Abbott sat on the sofa and watched television for a while, then Alice switched it off.

'Why do the heroes always hit the villains but the villains never hit the heroes? With bullets, I mean.'

'Because the heroes are better shots, sweetheart. Besides, what would happen to the series if someone put a bullet through Kojak's bald head?'

'But it's got nothing to do with real life.'

'Who wants real life, which is nasty, brutish and short, after a lousy day at the office or the factory or whatever? All they want are myths. And why not?'

'All I want is a coffee. You?'

'Fine.'

'Let's have it in the kitchen. I like having coffee in the kitchen.'

They had coffee in the tiny kitchen, sitting on opposite sides of the tiny table.

She jerked her head towards the canary.

'You know Solomon?'

Abbott nodded. 'We have met.'

'He used to sing like mad. All the time. Now he never sings a note.'

'Perhaps he's got a frog in his throat.'

'I used to think it might be something to do with you. It was about the time you went to Africa that he stopped singing. I thought he might start again now you're back.'

'I'm not sure I follow the logic of that. Unless he fell madly in love with me.'

'It's nothing to do with logic. I just had the feeling that once he started singing again it'd be a good omen. And now you're back, which *is* a good omen, I thought he'd start singing. Don't you see?'

'Oh yes. Yes, of course,' Abbott said, not seeing at all.

She looked at the bird. 'Then *sing* Solomon, sing something.'

But the canary merely spread its wings, preened itself and stayed silent.

'And don't make any cracks about the Song of Solomon.'

'You're touchy tonight.'

She sipped her coffee, smoothed her hair back.

'You don't love me, do you? I mean, you're not *in* love with me. There is a difference.'

He took his time answering. 'I know I like you. You mean a lot to me. But I don't think about you all the time or want to write sonnets to your eyebrow. But what the hell, what do words mean anyway?'

'A lot to a woman.'

'They always sound so phoney coming from a man. Look, I like being with you, having you around, and' – almost with reluctance – 'I don't want to lose you.'

She looked down as she did habitually. Her heart suddenly felt too big for her chest. It was the first time in her life she had felt almost loved by a man, and she was unable to speak.

After a time he said, 'I have to make some phone calls tomorrow, then I have to go out.'

He finished his coffee. 'I may not be back for a day or two. But by then it'll be all over.'

'Maybe I'll go and see my mother tomorrow,' she said.

'That might not be a bad idea.'

Her hair had fallen forward again and she smoothed it back behind her ears.

'Tomorrow,' she said. 'And tomorrow and tomorrow.' She shook her long hair loose again. 'Will there be a tomorrow – for you and me?'

He was about to say I hope so or maybe or with luck when he suddenly realised she was on the edge of tears.

'Of course there will be,' he said, trying to soothe her with the warmth and confidence of his voice. 'But not here.'

'You don't mean South America, with all those war criminals?'

'No,' he said, smiling, 'not South America. Another country.'

'Where we'll be safe?'

'And live happy ever after.'

'Don't joke about it – please.'

She was on the edge of tears again. He leaned forward and took her face in his hands.

'When I walk you through the palm trees of Shaar hagolan,' he said, 'ask me if I'm joking.'

He touched her lips with his, then released her and leaned back.

'But why talk about the future? The present's pretty good, isn't it?'

'The present's wonderful,' she said, feeling as if the sun had come out in the middle of the night. 'What shall we do with it? Go to bed? Or are you too tired?'

'That's an insult, you ought to be slapped.'

'Promises, promises, promises,' she said, and for the first time that day laughed.

Doris was flown by helicopter to Leyfield Hall after dark and dined with Njala on Ogen melon (he wasn't anti-Zionist about anything that went into his belly), trout with almonds, roast duckling followed by biscuits and cheese, during which they finished the wine, a Clos de Bèze, and finally strawberries and cream drunk with a lightly chilled Monbazillac.

The meal, the wine, the setting and the service, which was as discreet as the lighting, went to Doris's simple head.

'You're fantastic,' she said, 'bloody fantastic.'

'Let us have coffee and Armagnac and go to bed.'

Which they did. And delighted each other. Doris wasn't a whore because she'd been deprived of money or a good home. She was a whore by vocation.

She gave Njala everything he wanted and more. They made love in every way a man and woman can make love, with side-variations they invented as they went along (or imagined they invented). What particularly pleased Njala was Doris's obvious enjoyment of it. Most women, after the first hour or so, put up with it. Not Doris. She loved every moment. Njala had to consume enormous quantities of Weetabix to keep up with her.

'There's only one thing I don't like,' she said.

'What's that?' he said in faint alarm.

'All this bloody Weetabix and no champagne.'

'Nothing could be simpler, my flower.'

He picked up the phone and said, 'Arthur, bring us half a dozen bottles of the Heidsieck, will you? And bring it yourself.'

'Here, wait a minute, we're bloody starkers.'

'My dear, ignore him as I assure you he will ignore us. He's a servant, a tool, an *instrumentum mutum*. Lie back and relax.'

Arthur brought in the champagne, opened a bottle, poured two glasses and left.

'Blimey, he never even looked at us.'

'Drink your champagne, my flower, and have some more Weetabix.'

It was a great night for Njala. He would never have a greater.

Alice and Abbott made love lingeringly and tenderly and passionately, sometimes making little sexual jokes that wouldn't have seemed nearly so funny to anyone else.

Then they lay back and shared a cigarette in a darkness lit only by splashes of moonlight.

'Am I making things difficult for you?' he said.

'What do you mean?'

'Divided loyalties, for instance. To the Department. To me.'

'All my loyalties are to you.'

'That's not quite true.'

'Anyway, I'm used to leading a double life – one real, the other a dream.'

'Which one is this?'

'The dream of course. But played for real.'

'Isn't that confusing?'

'Not for me. Not now, especially. Here, give us a drag, you're hogging it all.'

'Why not now?'

'Because now I'm living. And I mean *living*.'

'And no longer worried about tomorrow?'

'To hell with tomorrow. Sufficient unto the day.'

'And the night.'

'The night is made for loving, as someone said.'

'Not for sleeping, it seems. Except when you die. Then it's one long sleeping, as someone else said.'

'I know, I did it for A Levels. Wait a minute. . . . Nox est perpetua . . . something or other . . . dormienda.'

He offered her the cigarette back.

'No, you finish it.'

He took a couple of drags on it, watched the lighted end glow brighter.

'You don't resent me in any way? Resent my exploiting you, I mean.'

She smiled in the dark.

'You're not exploiting me. And anyway if you are that's fate or something – like tomorrow.'

'And tonight is made for loving,' he said and stubbed the cigarette out and took her in his arms again.

After a time he pulled her on top so that she sat astride him.

'Mmmm,' she said, 'I like this. Mmmm, it's nice. But everything with you is nice.'

In that moon-splashed darkness he could see little more of her than a silhouette, and the long hair falling down over her arms and shoulders.

'Did I ever tell you your arms and shoulders are beautiful?'

'I never knew anything about me was beautiful. Maybe it's the dark.'

'It's not the dark.'

She drew in her breath sharply. 'God, I wish this could last forever. I like the dark, then I can look at you and you can't see my funny eyes.'

'I can see the black ant on the black rock in the black night. And I like your eyes.'

She leaned down very close to him so that her long hair hid both their faces.

'If I live to be a hundred,' she whispered, 'I don't think I'll ever be happier than I am at this moment.'

He liked to sit on the verandah in the flush of dawn and watch the white mist from the mangrove swamps roll up over the town like a shroud and hang there, swirling in the light airs, till the sun came up and burnt it away and the dusty black-winged vultures settled on the tin roofs, looking like obscene lawyers waiting for briefs.

He spent most of his days gently sweating in the shade of the verandah, waiting for a cargo-boat to take him back to England.

With any luck he should arrive there within a few days of Njala, who was presently at an OPEC conference in Geneva whose objectives were to jack up the oil price to the Western countries still more and provide a lavish junket for the delegates.

Njala had a tight schedule over the following weeks. After Switzerland he would fly to Kampala for a meeting of the Organisation of African Unity (and another junket), then on to Beirut officially for a week's rest before going to London, but really for a secret meeting with leaders of the Black September terrorist group, which he supported with money and other help.

He was due in England at the end of April and so was the cargo boat, but cargo boat schedules are the reverse of tight and if Abbott's luck was out he might miss him. But it would make no difference in the end. He would follow him wherever he went, like the eye of God.

20

MONDAY broke mild and clear and again they had breakfast by the window in yellow sunlight. Both were silent. Then suddenly they had a row over nothing, over a piece of toast.

Abbott had had a piece of toast and three cups of coffee and Alice said he must have something more than a piece of toast and Abbott said he didn't want anything more and all of a sudden there was this row over a piece of toast – and there they were shouting at each other like a married couple.

Then Alice burst into tears and he took her in his arms and they both quietened down under the comfort of touching each other.

'It's today, isn't it?' she said.

He nodded. 'If it works out.'

'What do you mean?'

'Anything can sod up the plans of mice and men – from a flat tyre to a loud sneeze.'

'Then what do you do?'

'Try to put things right and hope to Christ they won't go wrong again.'

He still had her in his arms.

'Let go of me,' she said. 'Or hold me for ever.'

He let go of her and she reached up and kissed him formally on the cheek, like a wife.

'I hate goodbyes,' she said.

'Yeah.'

There was a brief silence, then she said, 'I'd better be getting off to my mother's. Will you be wanting the car?'

He shook his head. She went to the door.

'It's funny,' he said, 'how you spend half your life saying thank you and when you really want to say it . . . there's nothing to say.'

'Just come back to me,' she said and went out.

He listened to her going downstairs, then went to the window that overlooked the street.

He watched her walking away from him till she was out of sight. She didn't look back.

Then he went to the table, picked up the phone and dialled New Scotland Yard.

'Chief Superintendent Shepherd, please.'

He was asked to hold on, then a woman's voice said, 'Chief Superintendent Shepherd's office. Can I help you?'

'This is Department O-A-six,' he said giving the identifying code (and hoping they hadn't changed it during the past couple of years, though there was no reason why they should). 'Can I have a word with him?'

'He's down at Petersfield.'

'Oh, I thought he'd be up here after the shooting at Waterloo.'

'He was, but he went back.'

'Oh well, thanks.'

'Who shall I say called?'

'Mr Frank Smith's office.'

He rang off. So the safe house was at Petersfield. All he needed now was the address.

Njala took Doris for a walk round the grounds before seeing her on to the helicopter to London.

She was fascinated by the security that surrounded him.

'My God, all those dogs and men. They mustn't half think something of you.'

Njala laughed. 'Oh, it's all to do with a threat from the IRA or some terrorist group to kidnap visiting bigwigs. And the English are very security-minded.'

Wide-eyed she asked him all sorts of questions, which he answered with faintly patronising good humour.

Just before he left he said, 'I want to see you again. Soon.'

'When?'

'I can't say exactly, my schedules are subject to sudden

change. But I'll ring you – in a day or two at the latest. Make sure you're free.'

'You bet I will.'

In the flat Abbott was on the phone again, this time to one of the maintenance divisions that looked after the Department's houses in the south-east. He was speaking a fair imitation of a Welsh accent.

'Look, if you haven't done any maintenance there, boyo, how come I've got a work-sheet for renewing thirty foot of ogee guttering and repointing the bloody gable end? Tell me that. . . . No, I can't read the signature. But it's been passed and initialled by old Pilkington, see? So it must be all right, mustn't it? . . . Mystery? No mystery, boyo. Says here as plain as bloody daylight: "To work carried out at The Manor House, Updene, Petersfield". . . . What do you mean, wrong address? Don't tell me we haven't got a place at Petersfield because I know we bloody have. . . . Oh! Oh, that's it – Leyfield Hall. Here, you got the phone number handy, I don't want to go making a charlie of meself again. . . . Right. Thanks. But how come somebody in your division goes and puts the wrong bloody address on the work-sheet in the first place? All right, boyo, all right, it wasn't me that raised the query it was old Gimbel in Accounts – and you know what a bastard that bastard can be. . . .'

The phone rang and rang and rang and finally Doris woke up.

'Jesus,' she said into the phone.

'No, just George,' said Abbott.

'You know what time it is?'

'Five past one. In the afternoon.'

'I didn't get to bed till ten o'clock *this morning*. I'm shagged, George, shagged. . . . Boy, am I shagged.'

'We're in the money, baby.'

'Don't talk to me about money, George, just let me get back to sleep, will you?'

'For ten grand?'

'Ten what?'

'Forget it, baby, go back to sleep.'

'Listen, George, don't piss around, tell me straight.'

'I've set up a syndication deal with magazines in five countries – and there's ten big ones in it for you – if you come across with the goods. And if we can get a couple of pictures as well, add twenty-five per cent. But maybe you're not good at sums.'

There was silence at the other end of the line.

'You gone back to sleep, baby?'

'I'm getting wakier all the time. What do you want?'

'Meet me in that café on the corner of your street in a couple of hours.'

'Oh, shit, George, let's get some kip, will you? You know where I live. Come round here in a couple of hours – and I can talk laying down. I can do anything laying down.'

'Okay, okay,' Abbott sighed. 'Two hours, your place.'

She lived at the ribby end of Maida Vale. He caught a cab and was there in ten minutes, hammering on the door.

It was a safety precaution. Just in case she'd talked to the wrong people about her friend George. If the place was going to be staked out he wanted to be around to see it.

She opened the door with a sheet wrapped round her.

'Christ, you said two hours. I'm *dying*.'

'Ten grand'll raise you from the dead. I'll make you some coffee and you tell me about Njala and this place in the country.'

He made coffee and she talked. She told him everything she could about Njala's habits (not just the sexual ones) and the security arrangements.

She drew a sketch-plan of the house, the stream that ran through the grounds and the perimeter wall. She told him about the guard-dogs and their handlers, the electrified wire on the walls, the guards on the gate, the guards on the northern wall near the opening where the stream went through. She told him everything she could remember. Which was quite a lot.

'So there's no chance of slipping a photographer in?'

'No way, brother. They still search *me* when I go in. They got two dikey-looking policewomen in the house. Anyway, *he* still likes me. I'm going down there again.'

'When?'

'Dunno. Tomorrow or the next day, I guess. He's going to phone me.'

'See if you can get him to agree to having his photo taken with you. That'd be worth a bomb.'

'Okay, will do. And now, George, please, can I go back to sleep?'

He bought a light raincoat, an Ordnance Survey map of the Petersfield area, a packet of plastic bags of the kind used as pedal-bin liners, compass, screwdriver and a rubber-covered torch. He wasn't sure he'd need the torch, but it might come in handy.

At Waterloo Station he bought a paperback novel and took a single ticket to Petersfield. He became so absorbed in the novel he nearly went past his stop.

He made inquiries at a local estate agent's, saying he was interested in buying a country house with about twenty acres of land. Perhaps they could send him details of anything suitable. He gave them a fictitious name and address in London.

Friends had mentioned a local property some time ago that sounded interesting, but he couldn't remember the name. He frowned in thought. Leystone House, perhaps? Could that be it?'

'Ah, you mean Leyfield Hall,' said the agent. 'It was on the market about seven or eight months ago but has since been sold, I'm afraid.'

'It sounded interesting. Is it far from here?'

'No, only about two or three miles west along the A272. Big place standing back on the right. Can't miss it.'

Abbott studied the Ordnance Survey map, then took a cab and went past the main gates of Leyfield Hall. He noted the lodge (stuffed with armed Special Branch men, no doubt) and the archway in the wall where the stream came through. He also noted the position of the floodlights that would illuminate the archway after dark. According to Doris they weren't switched on till about nine – which was well after dark. The stream passed under the road and into some meadows. The banks were lined with trees which would provide adequate cover. After the stream came out of the archway it narrowed into a short deep ditch and passed under the road through an eighteen-inch drainpipe before widening out again into the meadow. No chance of getting through that drainpipe.

He took the cab on a network of minor roads that more or less encircled Leyfield Hall at distances up to twenty miles. He told the cabbie he was looking for land to buy. In fact he was looking for a large field preferably with a pond or stream in it. He found what he was looking for about twenty miles north-north-west of Leyfield Hall, according to the Ordnance map. A large flat field with a stream running through it – perhaps the same stream that ran through the grounds of the Hall.

At one point the stream widened out or had been deliberately widened to make a drinking-pool for cattle. The gleam of that pool in the dark would make an excellent landmark.

He noted the position of another landmark, a church spire about a mile away, and almost directly behind it the ruins of a castle. He checked their bearings with the compass, then noted the position of Leyfield Hall on the map and marked the position of the field and its stream.

So all he would have to do was fly north-north-west from the Hall till he saw the church spire with the ruined castle beyond, then follow his compass bearing to the field. The gleam of water would identify it.

There were one or two other preliminary things to do, and the first was to steal a Post Office van.

He found one in a car park near Petersfield station. The door was locked, but he forced the quarter-light with the screwdriver and managed to reach the release button. He got in, pulled the wires away from the ignition switch and tied them together. This turned the engine over but she wouldn't start without the choke. She was a little cold.

He drove her to a lane near the field with the stream and hid her just off the road in some bushes.

He knew the theft would be reported to Shepherd at Leyfield Hall. All crimes or suspicious actions in the area, however trivial, would be reported to him. That was the way Shepherd worked, and his unrelenting collection of detail was one of his strong points. Abbott believed that a man's strong points, as in judo, should be used against him.

He started to walk back to Petersfield and after a mile managed to hitch a lift the rest of the way. Not that he was in a hurry. There was nothing much he could do before dusk. Dusk's a funny time, a dangerous time. A time, for instance, that car-drivers, in England anyway, ignore. It is a time when it is difficult to decide if objects are stationary or moving, alive or dead. An in-between time. A time for lovers because they are always in between times except when together.

Njala rang Doris well before dusk.

'I'll have an embassy car take you to the heliport and you can be here in an hour.'

'But you said tomorrow or the next day. I've only just got up. I'm half-dead.

'I tell you what you do : you come down here, you have some smoked salmon and a bottle of champagne. Then you go to bed for two hours, three hours if you like. And when you wake up, all nice and fresh, you have a bath and. . . .'

'No, love, I can't, honest. I'm coming apart at the seams.'

'And there will be a little present of five hundred pounds for you.'

'Oh *hell*.'

Just before dusk Abbott went into a hotel and rang the Petersfield telephone exchange.

'I want to report a fault on Petersfield 8548. Yes, that's right. It's a Ministry of Defence priority line, so could you attend to it right away, please? Thank you.'

He took a cab to within half a mile of Leyfield Hall, slipped into the meadow and, keeping under cover, made his way through the trees and bushes along the bank of the stream till he found a place where he could hide but still have a good view of the main gates and the lodge.

Dusk was dropping now but the floodlights would not be switched on for at least half an hour, according to Doris.

Abbott wrapped his watch, his compass, his gun, the holster and a spare clip of ammunition in plastic bags, which he secured tightly with wire fasteners and stuffed into the pockets of his raincoat. Then he waited.

Within about ten minutes a Post Office van drew up at the main gates and honked.

The gates opened and three Special Branch men came out, led by the bright Sergeant Roberts.

The van driver, a thick-set aggressive-looking young man, wound down the window.

'Yes?' said Roberts.

'Telephone,' said the driver. 'You reported a fault on the line up at the house.'

'Just a moment, please.'

'I haven't got all bleed'n night.'

'Won't keep you a moment, sir.'

He turned to one of the other Special Branch men and said in a low voice, 'Check with the house.'

The driver got out of the van.

'Look,' he said, 'this *is* supposed to be an emergency, Ministry of Defence priority line or something. And I want to get out of here as quick as I can, see? I got a date. With a bird.'

The other Special Branch man came back and whispered something into Roberts's ear.

'Would you mind stepping into the lodge for a moment, sir? There are one or two questions we'd like to ask you.'

'Questions? What questions? What are you talking about?'

'A van answering this description was stolen this afternoon.'

'Stolen? You suggesting this van was stolen? Look at the number-plates, you great berk.'

'Easy enough to change number-plates, sir. Now, would you mind stepping this way?'

Roberts already had a hand on his arm.

'Yes, I bloody would,' said the driver, jerking free. The other two Special Branch men closed with him.

As all three hustled him, still struggling, through the gates. Abbott slipped across the road in the deepening dusk and slid down into the narrow ditch leading to the archway. The water was icy.

He moved very carefully and slowly up to the archway and examined it carefully. Embedded in the brickwork on either side of the arch about an inch or so above the water-line were two electronic eyes, as Abbot had expected.

He took a deep breath, ducked under the water and crawled along the muddy bottom till he was clear of the archway. Then he surfaced and climbed silently out of the stream into the shelter of some bushes. He dried his hands on a handkerchief and waited till he had stopped shivering. Then he took his compass, watch, gun, holster and ammunition out of their plastic bags, which he weighted with stones and put into the stream. Perhaps he was being overcautious, but he was a very cautious man. He took the raincoat off and hid it under a bush and covered it with leaves.

He strapped on the holster and examined the gun and the ammunition carefully. Both were dry. So were the watch and the compass. He slipped the gun into its holster, the ammunition and the compass into his pocket, strapped the watch to his wrist.

He crept along the bank of the stream, keeping to the bushes and lying still when he heard a dog patrol approach. Once he had reached the rhododendrons lining part of the gravel forecourt in front of the house he lay and waited for the next dog patrol to pass. They went by at about fifteen-minute intervals, Doris had said.

Good old Doris.

He was now about a quarter of a mile from the bushes where he had hidden the raincoat. In the distance he heard a dog bark and wondered if it had found the coat. Then other dogs took up the barking.

In the summer-house Sergeant Clifford said to a Special

Branch man who had just come in, 'Something's up – and they don't like it.'

'They bark at any bloody thing. Besides there's a bit of aggro at the main gate.'

There was a short silence, then more barking. One of the dogs could be heard howling.

'I don't like it either,' said Clifford. 'I'm going out to have a butcher's.'

From the rhododendrons Abbott watched Clifford circle the house. Then a dog patrol went by. Clifford exchanged a few words with the handler, then returned to the summer-house.

By now the dogs had stopped barking and howling. But even the silence bothered Clifford. There seemed to be a sort of sinister expectancy about it.

'Something's up,' he said. 'I don't know what the bloody hell it is, but something's up.'

'Feel it in your water, can you? said the Special Branch man, who didn't like Clifford. Hardly anyone did.

As soon as Clifford and the dog patrol were out of sight Abbott crossed the gravel forecourt quickly, ran up the three steps to the massive oak front door – and rang the bell.

The door was opened by Shepherd.

'Good evening,' Abbott said politely.

Shepherd found himself looking down the barrel of a Combat Magnum .357, held in a very steady hand. It would have chilled a braver man than Shepherd – and he was no coward.

Abbott stepped inside, closed the door behind him.

'Give me your gun,' he said. 'With two fingers, you know, just like they do on the telly.'

Shepherd gave him the gun, which he put in his pocket.

'Now let's go up to Njala's suite. I'll be about two paces behind you, so don't try that unarmed-combat trick they teach you on all those courses, unless you want a shattered spine.'

Shepherd went upstairs like a man stepping on thin ice. Abbott followed.

The Special Branch guard who was sitting on a chair by the entrance to Njala's suite saw Shepherd and that someone was following behind him. He did not see the gun – till Abbott told Shepherd to move aside.

'Don't be brave, son,' Abbott said. 'Just stand up and keep still.'

The Special Branch man did as he was told.

'Take his gun and his handcuffs and give them to me,' Abbott told Shepherd. 'And whatever you do don't make me nervous.'

Shepherd took the gun and handcuffs and gave them to Abbott.

'Move well away from the door, gentlemen – and no drama, please.'

They moved away. Abbott went to the door and listened. He didn't want Njala alarmed. Then he turned and stepped delicately towards Shepherd, measured his distance and with explosive suddenness kicked him in the solar plexus.

Shepherd gasped like a balloon losing air and sank to the floor with hardly a sound, just that strangled gasping as he fought for breath and his face turned a dirty shade of mottled blue.

Abbott leant over him.

'My wife,' he said softly, 'wished to be remembered to you.'

He went to the door, listened again, then opened it and went in. He shut the door quietly behind him and locked it

Njala was working at his desk by the west window. He did not look up. He was absorbed in his work and though he knew someone had entered he paid no attention. He did not even hear the door being locked, or if he did the significance did not register.

'Put it down on the side table, Arthur, and pour yourself a cup.'

He went on working.

After a moment Abbott said, 'I am not Arthur.'

Njala looked up, saw the man, saw the gun.

'You must be Wilson,' he said. 'Or the one we know as Wilson. The one who's come to kill me.'

He paused, half-smiled.

'What can I do for you?' he said. 'Apart from dropping dead?'

Whatever qualities Njala lacked, courage wasn't one of them.

'Pull the blind down.'

It was getting dark outside and Njala already had the lights on.

While Njala pulled the blind down over the west window, Abbott did the same for the south windows. He didn't want anyone looking in from the outside.

'Sit down and keep both hands on the desk.'

Njala did so. In the middle drawer of the desk was a gun. With painful slowness he began to tease it open with his knee. At the same time he kept talking to cover any slight noise the drawer might make.

'Would you like a drink?' he said brightly. 'Gin, whisky, vodka, anything . . . ?'

'Nothing,' said Abbott. 'Not even a glass of water.'

21

WITHIN a few minutes Shepherd had recovered his breathing and most of his colour. He had a purple bruise on his belly and an aching gut that caught him like a knife if he breathed deeply or made an awkward movement.

He phoned the Controller, who phoned the Minister and Smith, telling Smith to have an RAF helicopter standing by at the London Heliport as soon as possible, preferably sooner.

The Controller then phoned Shepherd back.

'Can you talk to him?'

'Of course. On one of the extension phones.'

'Then talk to him. And stall.'

'How?'

'I don't know. Tell him I want a word with him. Tell him I'll be down in half an hour. And for Christ's sake don't try any tricks.'

The Controller could hardly know that Shepherd was not in the mood for tricks as he sat by the phone sadly rubbing his aching belly and trying to keep his breathing shallow. The prospect of an early retirement, which he had once spurned, grew more attractive with each painful breath.

He spoke to Abbott, trying to keep the hate out of his voice.

Yes, Abbott would wait for the Controller if in the meantime Shepherd managed to get a helicopter to the house – not one of the big RAF types but a small two-seater. He wanted it landed on the forecourt in front of the house and as near the steps as possible. He also wanted it surrounded with flood-lights pointing away from the helicopter.

'I'll do my best, but choppers don't grow on trees. And where would I get one of those two-seater jobs?'

'That's your problem. But get it. And start fixing up those

floodlights now. But don't switch 'em on till I tell you.'

Abbott had no intention of waiting for the Controller. If the two-seater helicopter arrived first he would take it – and Njala with him.

Shepherd gave instructions to move the floodlights to the forecourt, then went to the summer-house. He walked slowly and back on his heels like a pregnant woman. He was beginning to feel like one too, only worse.

'So he's done it, the bastard's done it,' said Clifford bitterly. 'If I'd've gone out for my look-around a couple of minutes later I'd've got him.'

'Or alternatively,' said Shepherd, 'he'd have got you.'

Njala was playing it the only way he could – cool. And still trying to ease that desk drawer open a millimetre at a time.

'You were sent to kill me once before, weren't you? By your government.'

'You knew?'

'It wasn't very hard to work out. They'd bought most of the secret information they wanted – our officials are very corrupt, I'm afraid. So what else was there? Except murder.'

'My masters called it assassination. It was only later they called it murder.'

'What do you call it? Execution? Justifiable homicide?'

Abbott shrugged. 'Does it matter?'

'Only insofar as it has to be justified once more – even to me, the victim.' The drawer was now open at least an inch. 'Which, as Euclid would say, is absurd.'

Keep talking to them, get them relaxed, make friends with them as far as possible. That was the technique with terrorists, but of course Abbott would know about that technique too.

'I wasn't aware your death needed justifying.'

'It didn't once – when you were first sent to kill me. Then you'd have shot me on sight, with the silent approval of your government. Now you no longer have that approval. Or anyone's approval.'

Abbott smiled one of his small smiles. 'I have my own approval.'

'Then why don't you shoot me instead of talking about it? Ah, of course, the helicopter.'

Abbott nodded. 'That's right. I'm going to take you somewhere else and shoot you.'

'That might set you problems.'

'I've solved them so far.'

'Oh yes, you're a resourceful man. May I?'

He pointed to a cigarette-box on the desk.

'As long as there's not a gun in it.'

Njala opened the box so that Abbott could see it contained nothing but cigarettes.

'Something just as lethal, I'm told.'

'You won't die of it.'

The Controller, the Minister, the belly-rubbing Shepherd and Smith, who had to suppress a tendency to smile whenever he looked at Shepherd, were in conference in the summer-house. Clifford was as motionless as a spider, watching the lighted west window.

'How the hell he ever got past the main gate beats me,' said Shepherd.

'As easily as he got into the house, I expect,' said Smith.

'Now wait a minute, who'd've thought he'd walk right up and ring the bloody front-door bell? I mean, that's for official visitors.'

'Perhaps the poor bastard didn't know any better. You should've put a notice up.'

'Look, don't get smart with me—'

'The point is, gentlemen,' said the Controller, 'what are we going to do?'

'What *can* we do?' said the Minister. 'He's got us by the balls, hasn't he? Like a hijacker on a plane.'

A phone had been installed in the summer-house. The Controller pointed to it.

'Can I get him on this?'

'The switchboard in the house'll connect you,' said Shepherd.

The Controller picked the phone up.

'Put me through to President Njala's room.'

Abbott came on the line.

'Yes?'

'This is the Controller.'

'Have you got the chopper I asked for?'

'We've got one of those big RAF jobs.'

'I asked for a two-seater. And don't tell me they don't grow on trees. Get it.'

'I'm doing my best.'

'You don't imagine I'm going to wait till daylight, do you? I want it here while it's still dark. And I'll give you half an hour. From now. Otherwise Njala's a dead man.'

Abbott hung up.

'What does he want with the two-seater?' said the Controller. 'What's his plan?'

'I think I can tell you,' said Smith. 'With Njala as hostage he's going to fly a few miles to some place where he has a car waiting, with or without an accomplice, kill Njala – and then make his way back to his hide-out by a mixture of car, train, bus and whatever other form of transport he's dreamed up or manages to find available. He's a great improviser.'

There was another silence. Then the Minister said: 'How do we stop him? And stop him killing Njala?'

'The two-seater chopper will be here within half an hour,' said the Controller, 'so will a mobile radar unit. At least we'll be able to keep track of him.'

'He'll fly under the radar,' said Smith.

'Can't we follow him in another helicopter?' said the Minister.

'Not if you want to keep Njala alive and well,' said Smith. 'Anyway, he'll be flying without lights.'

'But if he's flying a helicopter himself he won't be able to hear another one, will he?'

'He'll hear it when he lands. And then Goodbye Njala.'

'But how will he land it in the dark?' said the Minister.

'During the war,' said Smith, 'I landed Lysanders in a damp field by the light of three paraffin flares. And a chopper's a bloody sight easier to land than a Lysander. Besides, there's a light directly under a chopper which he can switch on for a few seconds to gauge his height. And if he does make a clumsy landing and bends it a bit he's hardly going to burst into tears.'

'But while he's flying the helicopter, Njala surely will try to—'

'Njala will be handcuffed,' said Shepherd.

'So,' said the Minister thoughtfully, 'not to put too fine a point on it, we're buggered.'

'And Njala with us,' said Smith.

'Couldn't we,' said the Minister, 'just do nothing? You know, like they did with Herrema and the Spaghetti House job?'

'No,' said Smith, 'different motives. Abbott's not holding him for ransom. He's going to kill him anyway. Whether he himself dies or not. Of course if he *can* get away afterwards, he will. But the escape is secondary, the killing primary.'

'Oh my God,' said the Minister.

'We're dealing with a crackpot not a criminal,' Shepherd explained.

'I knew you'd have a brilliant phrase for it,' said Smith. 'How's your poor tum-tum?'

At that moment a man walked in whom the Controller introduced as Dr Rostal, the SIS psychiatrist who had examined Abbott. He was small and dark and round and looked like a Jew, which he was.

'Is there anything you can do?' said the Minister.

'No.'

'Then why did you come?'

'The Controller asked me to.'

'Can you advise us?' said the Controller.

'I don't know.'

'What *do* you know,' said the Minister, 'if anything?'

Rostal turned his black speculative eyes on the Minister, stared him down, then turned back to the Controller.

'According to our tests he was an intelligent man of action, very resourceful, with a quite remarkable degree of determination. An ideal subject from our point of view. Or almost ideal.'

'Almost?' said the Minister.

'I did point out that he had a conscience, a moral sense. And an assassin should perhaps be totally amoral.'

'There,' said the Minister, anxious to blame someone. 'Why the hell *did* you pick him? If you hadn't we wouldn't be in this mess.'

The Controller spoke slowly. 'I did not want to risk an amoral killer spraying bullets at the target and killing innocent bystanders as well – even if they were only a lot of nig-nogs.'

'Now look here,' said the Minister, his face changing colour, 'that was just one of my little jokes.'

'Anyway, Abbott was miles ahead of the other agents we tested, and was obviously the best man for the job.'

'I agree,' said Rostal. 'I was merely pointing out that in certain circumstances a moral sense can be a disadvantage.'

'That's why we had to morally justify the assassination to him,' said the Controller.

'I think,' said Smith, 'even at this distance, I can hear Abbott laughing. Or could it be God?'

'If you've no more questions for me,' said Rostal, 'I have a train to catch.'

'Can't you think of any way we might stop him?' said the Minister.

'Only with a bullet. Goodnight, gentlemen.'

After Rostal had gone Smith said softly, 'And goodnight Njala.'

'Do you realise the sort of international incident his murder will cause?' said the Minister. 'The effect on the Organisation of African Unity, on the oil sheikhs, on the situation in Africa and the Middle East?'

'I can think of a place in the Middle East where there might be mild rejoicing,' said Smith. 'Called Israel.'

'And what about the heads that will roll here?'

He wasn't thinking of heads. He was thinking of one head, his own.

'One man up there with a gun – and there's nothing, absolutely nothing we can do about it.'

There was a longish silence. No one was disagreeing with

him. Then the silent Clifford spoke. 'Only a bullet will stop him. That's what the man said.'

'Yes, yes,' said the Minister impatiently. 'Tell us something we don't know.'

'The window blind. Every once in a while it moves in the draught. Now, if I could find the right observation point – say, in one of those trees – I might get a glimpse of him. . . . It's all I'd need.'

There was another, longer silence.

Then Smith said, 'We wouldn't want a cock-up like the last time, would we, though?'

Clifford's pale face was without expression.

'The circumstances are quite different. All I have to do is wait till the blind moves and I can see him.'

'That's two quite separate things. The blind may move – but you still mightn't be able to see him.'

'Agreed, but all I can see from here if the curtain moves is a bit of the ceiling. But if I was in the right observation point I could see into the room.'

'Into a part of the room – where he might or might not be.'

'Agreed again. But there's just a chance he might be where I could get a glimpse of him. Just a chance.'

'We've still got twenty minutes before the deadline runs out,' said the Minister. 'And even then we might be able to stall him a bit longer. . . . Anyway, I think it's a chance worth taking. Almost any chance is worth taking at this point.'

He turned to the Controller. 'What do you think?'

'I don't know. It might work, I suppose.'

'Shepherd?'

'It's about the only chance we've got.'

'Smith?'

'No.'

Another of those silences.

'What's your objection?' said the Minister.

'There are too many unknowns in the equation – as Abbott once said to me.'

'Explain yourself.'

'If Clifford finds the right observation spot. If the blind

moves at the right time – that is, when Abbott happens to be in the line of fire. And finally *if* Clifford hits him.'

Clifford stood up and turned from the window for the first time.

'If I hit him? *If* I hit him?'

'Okay, you'd hit him. You'd hit him all right. But would you hit him in a vital spot? Would you, in other words, be able to stop him shooting Njala?'

'Listen,' said Clifford, 'if I hit him with that boat-tailed bullet *any*where he won't be in a condition to shoot anyone. That bullet makes a small entry hole but leaves an exit wound up to four inches square. And if it only hits his little finger it'll knock him down.'

'And I'll have half a dozen armed men bursting into the room,' said Shepherd, 'the moment they hear a shot.'

Smith nodded. 'Great,' he said. 'Great. Everything's perfect.'

'Except?' said the Controller.

'I don't know,' said Smith. 'Except nothing ever goes as planned. What's that saying about God always answering your prayers – but never to the foot of the letter?'

'Frank,' said the Controller, 'we're not talking about certainties, we're talking about chances, that's all. Clifford's way gives us a chance. Maybe not much of a chance. But a chance. Can you think of a better?'

Frank Smith sighed. 'No,' he said. 'I can't. Christ, I could do with a drink.'

'It's funny,' said Shepherd, 'how neurotics always turn to drink in a crisis.'

'Yes,' said Smith, 'it's one of the things that differentiates us from perverts and policemen. Can I speak to him?'

'Abbott?' said the Controller. 'Of course.'

Smith picked up the phone.

'Put me through to Njala's room.'

After a moment there was a click.

'Abbott here.'

'Richard, I just realised I mightn't get a chance to talk to you again and I wanted to . . . wish you luck or whatever.'

'You're not supposed to wish the wrong side luck.'

'You know you haven't got a cat in hell's chance of coming out of this alive?'

'Cats take a lot of killing, I'm told. Even in hell.'

'Is there nothing any of us can say or do to make you . . . change your mind?'

'Nothing, Frank.'

Smith hesitated, reflected. 'Then you may as well know that Njala helped kill those people in Trafalgar Square. He smuggled the bomb in for Black September. They gave him that nice gold bracelet in memoriam—'

The Minister snatched the phone from his hand, banged it down.

'What the hell are you doing, putting another nail in Njala's coffin?'

'What does it matter? He's going to be buried anyway.'

22

NJALA was still teasing the drawer open with his knee. He could see half the gun but that wasn't enough. He doubted if the whole gun would be enough. He'd need something else, a diversion, a distraction: and the way Abbott was staring at him now, like a snake about to strike, it would take an earthquake to distract him.

The coldness of that unwavering stare began to worry him, began to make him feel cold himself, or so he imagined, and he wasn't an imaginative man.

'I can understand your bitterness,' he said, 'your desire to kill me. You are not alone in that. But is it your only motive? Is it only personal – or is it political as well?'

Abbott continued to stare at him.

'If it's political there's not much hope. Anyone who risks his life in a political cause is a fool. And you can't argue with fools. But if it's personal . . . well, despite all the emotion, an understanding might be reached . . . compensation might be arranged. Of some sort. Indeed, of any sort.'

Abbott was only half-listening. His faculties were fully employed watching Njala, watching the windows, listening for the helicopter, though he did wonder idly why Frank Smith had told him about Black September. An indirect way of showing his disapproval of the Establishment? Or was it simply to harden Abbott's resolve? He smiled to himself. As if it needed hardening.

'What are you smiling at?'

'I was wondering where you got that beautiful gold bracelet.'

Despite the fact that he felt cold, Njala began to sweat. But Abbott didn't pursue the subject.

In the summer-house it was finally decided to let Sergeant Clifford see if he could find a vantage point. And he soon did – a nicely spreading tree almost opposite the west window.

He also found a near-perfect crotch to take the barrel of his beautiful rifle. All he had to do now was wait for the blind to move. And pray, which came easily to him. He was a naturally religious man.

Njala could see at least half the gun. He could even grab it if he wanted to commit suicide. He continued his patient efforts to open the drawer – and to keep the conversation going.

'You're an old-fashioned liberal, did you know that? Well, all liberals are old-fashioned. Radicals without a cause. Exploited by the Left, despised by the Right.'

He paused, waiting for comment. None was made.

'What am I, you may ask. Dictator? Fascist? Communist? Pick your own label. You will anyway.'

The drawer squeaked.

'What was that?'

The Combat Magnum was pointing at Njala's heart, as unwavering as the eyes behind it.

'I think it's this chair. It creaks sometimes.'

Abbott apparently accepted the explanation. The gun was lowered. Njala, who had been holding his breath, breathed again.

Abbott picked up the phone. 'Put me through to the Controller.' A moment later the Controller came on the line.

'Your precious friend has twelve minutes to live if that chopper doesn't show up,' Abbott said and put the phone down.

'Twelve minutes. It doesn't seem very long to live.'

'Give me one reason why you should live longer.'

'My country needs me.'

Abbott started to smile. Njala moistened his lips.

'A country gets the leader it needs at the time it needs him. Otherwise it's done for. And at this time my country needs me '

'To kill and torture?'

'Brutality is sometimes necessary, especially at our present stage of development. I control it. I contain it. If I tried to do away with it altogether, it would be taken as a sign of weakness. And I'd be out. And civil war would be in.'

'Every villain rationalises his villainy.'

'I wouldn't know about that.'

He ran a hand through his crinkly hair. He was talking for his life and knew it. If he could keep Abbott interested even for a minute or so past the deadline . . . well, you never know. A chance is a chance is a chance is a chance, however slender.

And the drawer was nicely open now.

'What I do know is this : it's taken you, the British, a thousand years of more or less stable government to evolve a very imperfect form of democracy. And you expect us to do it in five minutes. Oh, you helped us. You also exploited us. Then you cleared out and left us with a constitution that doesn't work.'

'It doesn't?'

'Not for us. It's too sophisticated. We're not ready for it. We've got to go through our own forms of feudalism and capitalism and socialism and corruption and God-knows-what.'

'What has that to do with your viciousness?'

'I'm shaped by my environment, as we all are. And let me add that it's no more vicious than Elizabethan England – which you call the Golden Age. Or the mighty Victorian era. Sixty glorious years. Ever seen the child-prostitution figures for 1875?'

There was a long silence. Then Abbott smiled, not one of his small sad smiles, but a real one. It was so pleasant and friendly that Njala, relieved, smiled back.

'You know,' Abbott said, 'in the end all this chat about ethics and morality and comparative history comes down to bullshit. The real reason I came here to kill you is a lot simpler than that : you're a bastard and I want to kill you. And I'm going to kill you.'

For the first time Njala was frightened.

23

Twice the blind of the west window moved in the draught and Clifford caught a glimpse of the room. But all he saw of Abbott was part of his left arm. He hesitated. If it had been the right arm, which controlled the gun hand, he would have taken the chance. Especially as the Special Branch men would burst into the room in seconds. But the left arm. . . . He sighted on it. It would certainly knock him over – and the Special Branch men would certainly do their stuff fast enough. But if it didn't come off – if Abbott *did* get time to pull the trigger. . . . Christ, he couldn't afford another balls-up. Then the curtain moved again, revealing a little more of Abbott's left arm. If it moved even a fraction more and revealed the shoulder, Clifford would fire. It would take half his shoulder away and he'd never have time for anything. He'd be flat on his back and too shocked to know if it was Christmas or Easter.

He lined up the cross-hairs of the night-sight and waited. And prayed again.

As he did so the helicopter ordered by the Controller swept past the window of the room where Doris was sleeping and landed on the lawn.

The clattering din of its great blade woke her up.

'For Chrissake,' she muttered.

The she heard voices from the other room and got up.

She yawned, wrapped a sheet round herself and went to the door to the sitting-room. It was already partly open.

Something about one of the voices – and it wasn't Njala's chesty rumble – was vaguely familiar.

The door was at a right incline behind Abbott so he didn't see her when she appeared in the doorway.

'George,' she said, 'what the—'

Abbott spun round. Njala jumped up, grabbed the gun out of the drawer and fired.

At that moment the curtain was back in place. All Clifford could see silhouetted against the blind was a man with a gun. He hesitated no longer, he fired.

The guns must have gone off almost simultaneously.

Njala's bullet, a 9mm from a Walther P38, hit Abbott in the chest.

Clifford's bullet took half Njala's head off and spattered his brains on the opposite wall.

The Special Branch men burst in but saw there was nothing they could do for anyone but Doris, who was having hysterics. One of them took her downstairs and left her in charge of a calm and sympathetic policewoman.

Smith, Shepherd and the Controller reached the room within seconds. Clifford followed a few moments later.

Abbott was still alive but haemorrhaging badly. He had been shot through the right lung. Smith went to him and supported him.

Abbott spoke with difficulty. 'The girl distracted me. And he shot me.' He pointed to Njala. 'He had a gun in the desk.'

He paused, pointed at Clifford.

'And he shot Njala.'

'All I saw was the silhouette of a man with a gun,' said Clifford. 'It had to be Abbott.'

'Shot him,' said Abbott, 'with the gun designed for the job. . . . Nice. . . .'

He tried to laugh but blood came into his mouth and he seemed to lose consciousness. Smith thought he was dead.

Then he opened his eyes again but Smith could see no recognition in them.

'Tell her . . . I'll walk her,' he said, his voice failing, 'walk her through the palm trees . . . of Shaar hagolan.'

'What?'

Smith cradled him in his arms.

'What did you say, Richard?'

Abbott's breathing became noisy and irregular. Then he caught sight of Clifford, tried to laugh again but choked on his own blood and died. The time was about half-past nine.

24

ALICE had deliberately stayed away from the radio and television all day.

She got home from her mother's about eight o'clock in the evening.

She was too tensed up to eat or to do anything except make cups of tea and walk around the flat.

She was waiting for something. A phone call. A ring at the door. A sign. An omen.

And then it came. At about half-past nine it came. And she knew everything was going to be all right.

Solomon started singing. And singing beautifully. More beautifully, more gaily, more poignantly than he had ever sung before.

Tears of joy started down her face.

And she sat there in that tiny kitchen, listening to the song of Solomon, waiting for Abbott to come back and kiss her with the kisses of his mouth and love her with the love that many waters cannot quench nor the floods overflow.